Horse Healer

Puzzle

Nothing about him seemed to balance properly. Even the tail was an odd, stubby-looking thing, as if someone had cut it once and it had never grown properly again. Hurriedly, Nicky ran a list of names through his head. He didn't want to call the horse anything plain or clumpy, but anything fancy or magical would sound wrong. If he didn't come up with something quick though, there was a chance Lynette might go for a cheap laugh, and hang some sort of joke name on him.

Suddenly it came to him. The funny patches. The odd-shaped body. The whole feeling that somehow the horse didn't quite fit. "Puzzle," he said. He looked Patty in the eye as he spoke. After all, it was only a white lie. "The owner said his name was Puzzle."

Horse Healer

Puzzle

Judy Waite

Hippo

For Richard

Scholastic Children's Books,
Commonwealth House, 1–19 New Oxford Street
London WC1A 1NU, UK
a division of Scholastic Ltd
London ~ New York ~ Toronto ~ Sydney ~ Auckland
Mexico City ~ New Delhi ~ Hong Kong

First published by Scholastic Ltd, 1999

Copyright © Judy Waite, 1999

ISBN 0 439 01008 X

All rights reserved

Typeset by
Cambrian Typesetters, Frimley, Camberley, Surrey
Printed by Mackays of Chatham plc

2 4 6 8 10 9 7 5 3 1

The right of Judy Waite to be identified as the author
of this work has been asserted by her in accordance with the
Copyright, Designs and Patents Act, 1988.

Author's Note

In writing this book, I owe a special "thank you" to Patrick Appleby of Botley Mill in Hampshire, who not only allowed me to explore his wonderful water mill, but also gave me ideas and information which actually changed the direction of the story.

1

"That's the oddest-looking horse I've ever seen." Nicky leaned on the gate, watching as the owner slipped a halter on to a gawky brown and white cob, and led him across.

Close up, the horse looked stranger than ever. His head seemed too big. His neck seemed too long. He had a patchy coat – odd brown splodges like pieces from a jigsaw puzzle amongst the white. Some of the colour seemed to trickle down under his belly and inside his legs, as if someone had thrown a can of paint at him. On his face, just over one side, ran a white mark that covered his left eye, then spread all the way down to his mouth. It gave him a lopsided, slightly confused expression.

Nicky unlatched the gate and swung it open for

Tom, the head groom at Mill Farm Riding School, and they walked through together, towards the horse.

"He looks like something from another planet. He'll frighten all the kids in the riding lessons on Saturday mornings. I don't think…" Tom began to joke, then broke off as a fit of coughing suddenly hacked through him. As the cough died, he bent stiffly, running his knotty, weathered hands over the horse's legs.

Nicky was standing at the front of the horse, rubbing his hand gently across the mottled brown fur on its forehead. The horse stood very still, watching him with dark, liquid eyes, the colour rich and warm like melted black chocolate. The eyes had a brightness – almost as if there was a light behind them – that seemed to shine through.

"He's very willing," the owner was saying. "You won't have any trouble with him." He gave a sharp jerk to the nose band, as if to prove that this was a horse who could take a bit of roughness. He wasn't a cruel man, but he was a dealer. He bought and sold horses, and he liked to sell them on quickly. This one was proving harder to shift than most.

Tom walked slowly all round the horse, checking him over. The horse sniffed him back, nuzzling in his pockets and suddenly pulling out a packet of peppermints with his teeth. Tom laughed, and gave him one. "He seems gentle enough. And he looks very fit. If I was buying him with my own money, his looks wouldn't be a problem, but we're not supposed to be pleasing ourselves here. What do you think, Nicky?"

Nicky's green eyes rested on Tom for a moment. He hesitated. He liked this horse, he had a good feeling about it, but he had to be careful too. This was the first time Tom had asked him to come out when he was buying a new horse. He knew Tom would respect his decision, but there was someone back at the yard who would be quick to criticize. "I need to try him. See how he goes."

The owner nodded. "I'll get the tack."

"Don't bother. I'll take him bareback. I won't need long."

Nicky sprang lightly on to the horse, then nudged him gently. The horse flickered his ears and stepped forward. He wasn't a comfortable ride. There was a stiffness about his movements that made him jerky. Nicky pressed him into a trot, and then a canter. The awkwardness was still there. Tom was right. With his odd looks and his uneven stride, he wouldn't be popular with the kids, and that was what they had to think about.

He walked the horse back to where the others were standing and slid off. Immediately the horse turned its head towards him and rubbed its nose against his arm. Nicky ran his fingers through the scraggy mane.

"What d'you think now?" Tom was coughing again. He looked tired suddenly, as if even trying to make a decision was hard work.

Nicky ran his hands through his dark hair and shook his head. The horse wouldn't do. Not for what they were looking for, at any rate. But just then, he caught the horse's eye again. It still held that same warm, liquid beauty, but this time the look seemed empty. Almost resigned. It was as if the light had gone out. Nicky didn't let himself think any more. He just said what he felt, the words almost tumbling out of him. "I think he's great. There's something about him. I think we should have him."

Within ten minutes the gawky skewbald cob was following Nicky quietly into the horse box, and Tom drove them back home to the yard.

2

Lynette, the deputy groom, came out of the office – which was really a converted stable – as soon as they arrived.

She watched as the brown horse followed Nicky out of the box and stood in the middle of the yard, looking around him with interest. "Not exactly an oil painting," she said at last.

"He was a good price…"

"There had to be *something* good about him." Lynette flicked a frizz of blonde fringe back from her face, and darted a glance to where Tom was shuffling up towards the main house to tell the stable owner, Patty Lake, they were home. His shoulders were hunched forward, and he was still coughing.

"He's got a gentle nature. He'll be good with nervous kids." Nicky wove a tiny plait into the horse's mane, trying not to sound irritated.

Lynette swung back round to face him, her blue eyes cold stones of disapproval. "I don't know what Tom was thinking of. He knows Patty's trying to build up a reputation as a quality school. This thing looks like he'd be more suited to pulling a rag and bone cart than teaching anxious little darlings to do rising trot. Still, I can see why he appealed to you."

This time Nicky's eyes flashed angrily. He knew what she was getting at. She was picking away at the fact that he was a Gypsy. He'd met lots of gorgios – people without Gypsy blood – who were like that.

Beside him, the horse blew gently on his neck. "Tom's the head groom here. He was happy to go with what I thought."

"If you ask me, Tom's losing his touch. He shouldn't even be taking you with him, let alone letting you make important decisions about what horses we buy. You're only here because he's got a soft spot for you. You don't even work here officially."

"I put in plenty of time. I just don't happen to get paid."

"Well, that makes you pretty stupid for a start."

"You used to do the same, before you left school last term."

"Not like you. Not for nothing. I was in training. Patty always promised me—" Lynette broke off suddenly, and looked round at the sound of footsteps. Patty Lake was hurrying towards them.

Lynette flicked her hair back again, and smiled brightly as she got near. "Hi, Patty. I'm just giving the new horse a check over."

"Tom's been telling me about it. He's staying back at the house. He's not feeling too good at the moment." Patty Lake ran her bony fingers along the horse's side. Nicky noticed, not for the first time, that her fingernails were bitten right down to her finger tips. It always struck him as strange for a woman her age. Dad was always going on at his sister Sabrina for chewing her nails, but Patty Lake was really old – much older than Dad, even.

"He looks a bit odd." Patty turned to Nicky as she spoke. "I was hoping you'd come back with something we could use at the shows. Something we could put a leading rein on to parade little kids about. Something that could help us drum up new business from any rich mums that might be watching."

Nicky ignored the smug, slanted glance from Lynette. "I think he's got a gentle nature. We'll be able to use him for beginners. He's going to be a horse we can trust."

The criss-cross of lines on Patty's forehead

deepened, and she bit her thumbnail, "Even so, he's not exactly a good advertisement." Then she sighed. "Anyway, we've got him now, and I suppose we can always sell him on if he doesn't earn his keep. What's his name?"

"I..." Nicky hesitated. It seemed terrible somehow that he didn't know. That the owner hadn't bothered to tell them. That he and Tom hadn't even asked. He turned to the horse and ran his hands along its neck. The horse leaned against him trustingly.

Nicky stroked the funny, blotchy coat, and stepped back slightly. Lynette was right about the oil painting bit. It was like he'd been made out of leftovers. Nothing about him seemed to balance properly. Even the tail was an odd, stubby-looking thing, as if someone had cut it once and it had never grown properly again. Hurriedly, Nicky ran a list of names through his head. He didn't want to call the horse anything plain or clumpy, but anything fancy or magical would sound wrong. If he didn't come up with something quick though, there was a chance Lynette might go for a cheap laugh, and hang some sort of joke name on him.

Suddenly it came to him. The funny patches. The odd-shaped body. The whole feeling that somehow the horse didn't quite fit. "Puzzle," he said. He looked Patty in the eye as he spoke. After all, it was only a white lie. "The owner said his name was Puzzle."

Patty nodded. "Well, that seems to suit him. Get him into a stable now, and I'll watch you riding him tomorrow, when he's had a chance to settle in a bit. Can you come over at about eight, before the Sunday rides get started?"

"I'll make sure I'm here."

"Good. I'll see what I think then." She ran a hand through her short, greying hair distractedly. "I'm going back to the house now. I said I'd run Tom home later if he's still feeling rough."

She turned and hurried away.

Lynette's smile was brittle. "I told you," she whispered. "This horse had better be good when you take him out tomorrow. If you ask me, the clock's already started ticking for him. Patty's going to see that you made the wrong choice. She's not going to want him around for long. Except I can't think who else would ever take him off our hands." She gave a short, thin laugh, then walked briskly up the yard after Patty.

Nicky stood for a moment and watched her go. Lynette was loving every moment of this. If she could get the knife in about him in any way, she would. And as he watched her catch up with Patty and begin to walk beside her, he had the feeling she might be about to give it an extra twist.

He turned back to look at the horse, who was still standing patiently behind him. "So – Puzzle – I'm sorry it's not been a great welcome for you, but it's good to meet you." He rubbed the spot between the horse's eyes again. Nicky had been around horses since he was born, and he knew this was a way to gain their trust. Over the years he'd got hundreds of horses of all sizes and temperaments to follow him around like lambs. He understood all the ways they liked to be touched, and spoken to. Some of it he knew by instinct; some of it he'd got from working with Grandad when they lived and travelled together; and some of it he knew through Gypsy secrets that were passed through from generation to generation.

Now Puzzle stretched out his neck, sniffed at Nicky's pockets, then nuzzled against his shoulder. Nicky sighed. He wasn't going to have to work very hard to gain this horse's trust. Puzzle already seemed to have made a best friend out of him. Nicky just hoped that he wasn't going to have to let him down.

3

Tom's bungalow was kilometres from anywhere, tucked away amongst fields, on the edge of a rutted, unmade road.

It wasn't even a proper building – it was really a converted railway carriage with just three rooms, and an outside toilet.

Behind it was an old water mill, gaunt and derelict. Maggie, a white swan, was sunning herself beside the quiet water that ran up to the cast-iron grilles that the river had once filtered through. Maggie was half tame. Tom had rescued her years before, when she still had the dusty grey feathers of a cygnet. She'd flown up and hit the power lines that were feeding a new housing estate a few fields away. Tom said she was one of the lucky ones – at least she'd survived – but her left wing was broken and it never healed properly. He campaigned for a while to try and get silver balls hung on the line for the birds to see, but it didn't get done. Maggie never strayed far from Tom's bungalow, and when he was outside she followed him around and guarded him as jealously as a dog.

A small group of deer fed lazily on the grass the other side of the river. They were Tom's "friends" too. When he worked outside they often wandered over and grazed near him, and during the winter he left hay and grain out for them to eat.

As Nicky glanced at them he saw them raise their heads, then skitter away suddenly behind the trees. A moment later a man in a dark suit walked out of the woods that ran along the back of the field. The path through the trees led all the way down to Mill Farm. Nicky frowned. The man didn't look like anyone who'd be coming to see Tom, but he didn't look dressed for a walk in the country either. He watched for a moment as the man stopped and looked around him, then wrote something in a notebook. Then, with a quick glance at his watch, he turned right, walking along the edge of the wood to the stile that led out on to the road. A moment later Nicky heard a car start up and drive away.

It obviously wasn't a visitor for Tom anyway.

Nicky leant his bike against the wall of the

bungalow. Over the years the white paint had peeled away to reveal the wooden frame of the carriage underneath. The damp had got in, and it was rotting in places. Along the outside edge of the wall clumps of weeds and nettles grew together in wild tangles.

The door to the bungalow was half open, and Nicky poked his head round to look in the kitchen. Tom's old corduroy hat and faded brown jacket were draped across the table, so Nicky knew he must be in somewhere.

Nicky walked in cautiously. He normally refused to go inside houses – even the idea of being in them made him panic – but he was always comfortable in Tom's place.

Everything seemed quiet. Usually Tom had the radio on, or soft classical music playing in the background, but today there was nothing but the *drip*, *drip*, *drip* from the tap on the kitchen sink.

Nicky tightened the tap, then walked on through into the gloom of the front room. "Are you home?"

Tom gave an answering cough. He was huddled in an ancient leather chair in one corner of the room. It was a warm June day, but he had a blanket pulled over him. The curtains were closed, and a weak shaft of sunlight crept through a gap at the edge, picking out the dust on the old oak table beside him.

"I went to find you when I'd settled the new horse, but Patty said she'd already run you home. I was worried about you."

"There's nothing to worry about. Just a bit of a cold on my chest. I'll be right as rain in a day or two." Tom coughed again, an endless, dry sound that seemed to wrench through his whole body. He looked small and frail, peering out from the blanket.

"I'll make some tea. You sound really rough." Nicky hovered anxiously. He hadn't known Tom long, but he really liked him.

They'd met when he was out cycling one day. One of the Mill Farm horses – a chestnut stallion called Blaze that was the stable's pride and joy – had got out of his field and was causing chaos on the road. Tom and Lynette were trying to catch him, but they weren't having much luck. Blaze, eyes wild and panicking, kept twisting and bucking away from them – until Nicky went up and asked Tom quietly if he could have a try on his own. Within five minutes Blaze was walking at Nicky's shoulder, his tail swishing lazily as he followed him through the gate into the field.

As they walked together back to the yard, Tom and Nicky had started talking. The age difference didn't seem to matter, and they chatted as if they'd known each other all their lives. For Nicky, Tom gave him the warm feeling he used to get from being

14

with his Grandad in the days when they all lived together. For Tom, Nicky seemed an echo of how he himself had been, a long time ago.

From then on, Nicky went to Mill Farm as often as he could. He was too young to get paid for working there, but he helped with the horses – especially the difficult ones – and got free rides in return. That was more than enough payment for him.

"What did they think of the horse?" Tom struggled to sit forward as Nicky carried over his tea.

Nicky hesitated. He didn't want Tom to be upset. "They think he's fine. Patty just wants to see me ride him tomorrow. I said he was called Puzzle."

Tom laughed, and the laugh turned into a kind of choke. "Good name," he said at last, as the cough wore away until it was just a thickness in his throat. Then he looked hard at Nicky. In the late afternoon light his usually tanned face seemed faded and grey, but his eyes were almost fierce as he said suddenly, "Sometimes you have to trust your instincts, and blow what everyone else thinks. If a thing feels right, then nine times out of ten it probably is, in the long run."

Nicky nodded, turning his own mug round in his hands. The handle was broken off, and the china was hot to hold. "I know that. It's just going to be a problem getting everyone else to think the same."

"Just keep with it," Tom insisted. "As long as you're sure, people will generally listen in the end." He put his mug down on the table in front of him, leaned his head back in the chair, and closed his eyes. Within minutes Nicky heard the harsh rasp of his breathing turn to snores.

Very quietly he rinsed the mugs out in the sink, then spent half an hour outside pulling up weeds and nettles, before he cycled home.

4

Sabrina was curled up in front of the telly when Nicky got in. She was watching *Crazy About Creatures*, a local wildlife programme that came on every Saturday after the news. He stood and watched with her for a moment. "So who are they saving this week?"

"Ssssh." Sabrina kept her eyes glued to the screen as the presenter, Aileen Forbes, held up a raggy brown duck, found with a pellet from a shotgun embedded in its wing.

"They ought to do one about the swans at Tom's place. That's a good local cause."

"Be quiet." Sabrina flashed her dark eyes at Nicky. "I'm trying to listen."

"*...so send in all your old postcards for us to recycle,*

and help us raise money to protect some of the animals that live in and around our home town. Remember — our wildlife, and our environment, is everyone's responsibility. And don't forget the poster competition. We'll be showing the winners at the County Show at the end of July…"

"It's not fair," Sabrina grumbled, twisting her thick brown hair into a plait. "They always choose things we haven't got. Nobody's ever sent me a postcard in my life."

"What do you think they should ask for? Old car tyres? Rusty supermarket trolleys? We've got plenty of those outside at the moment."

"Don't be stupid." Sabrina shook her hair free again, and threw a cushion across at Nicky. "Anyway, you're in big trouble. You were supposed to be going with Dad to help Annie Hobbs — that carpenter woman — rub some furniture down this afternoon. Mum had to go instead, because Jim's not feeling that brilliant. Dad was steaming when he left."

"I forgot all about it. I had to go and see a friend." Nicky got himself a can of coke from the fridge and drank thirstily, flicking the ring pull into the bin in the corner. "What's that funny smell?"

"Vanilla Musk perfume. My friend got it for me in town this afternoon." Sabrina puffed a spray of a sickly ice-cream odour into the room.

"It's disgusting. And Dad'll go nuts if he thinks you're wearing perfume. You know he thinks you're getting too fussy about yourself as it is."

Sabrina shrugged. "Don't tell him then."

"It's a bit hard to miss it, with that stink everywhere."

He went over to the trailer window, and looked out. The site was cleaner than it used to be. Jim, Dad's older cousin who lived in the trailer Nicky slept in, had bagged up a lot of the logs that were cluttering the place up, and cut away mountains of nettles and thistles. Mum was growing flowers in pots, bringing bright splashes of colour everywhere. It all looked better than when they first came, but you still couldn't stop the gorgios from dumping rubbish nearby, or disguise the derelict garages that ran along the edge of the site. And although the council tip across the road had a high fence around it, on hot days it smelt like rotten eggs.

Nicky's mind wandered back to Mill Farm Stables. He wondered how Puzzle was coping with being in a strange place. Nicky had fed him, and made sure he was eating well before he left. He couldn't have been feeling too bad. A nervous horse would have blown its food around, or refused to eat at all.

Crazy About Creatures finished, and Sabrina got herself a coke. Nicky was aware of her hovering

19

about, just behind him. "Do you get on with people at school better this term?" she blurted suddenly.

Nicky dragged his thoughts away from Puzzle. "I hang around with Bretta mostly. I still help her with that horse Eclipse when I'm not at Mill Farm. She's got her on long loan now, because the owner's gone abroad for a couple of years." It was strange, but since he'd met Tom, Nicky went to ride Eclipse less and less. Only last term she'd been the most important horse in the world to him.

"But you feel like you've got friends at school. Like they've accepted you at last?" Sabrina stood beside Nicky, splayed her fingers out on the window sill, and began painting a glittery orange polish on to her nails.

Nicky gave his younger sister a searching look. "It's not too bad. Why?"

Sabrina was about to answer when there was a rattle of engine, and Dad's pick-up rolled up outside.

"You'd better get that stuff off your nails," Nicky murmured. "Dad's got a face like thunder."

Without another word, Sabrina slipped away into the shower-room, and Nicky braced himself to face the storm.

5

"**B**ut I *have* to go. I always spend the day there on Sundays, and I promised Patty Lake I'd be there by eight."

"So she's pinning you down to time as well now. That's really what I call slave labour."

"It's not like that. I want to go. There's this new horse—"

"Don't give me all that stuff about horses again. We've agreed you can go to the stables provided it doesn't interfere with what we need here. I nearly lost some work – and my reputation – this afternoon. You know Jim's arthritis is playing up, and if Mum hadn't been able to step in for you—"

"He's right, Nicky." Mum went to the sink and began scrubbing at her hands. She looked tired and dirty, and strands of long dark hair were escaping from her usual neat braids. "I had a stack of washing here I was supposed to be getting on with, and it's all piled up waiting for me now."

Nicky pushed past them both and stormed outside. Neither of them would even try to understand. And it was always useless trying to explain anything to Dad, where horses were concerned. He only just about tolerated Nicky going to Mill Farm anyway.

Dad had a "thing" about horses. When he was a boy, his sister Ellie had been in a terrible riding accident. Grandad said Dad had been there and seen it all, and it had changed him for ever. Even now, over twenty years later, he still couldn't talk about what happened, or even mention Ellie's name.

And now he was going to stop Nicky from riding Puzzle tomorrow morning. Dad was insisting he went with him to work on a tree-clearing job first thing, and after forgetting about helping Annie Hobbs this afternoon, there was no way he was going to let Nicky out of it.

Nicky sat outside on an old lorry tyre, and stared out through the dusky evening. If he couldn't ride Puzzle, then no doubt Lynette would do it, and there were no prizes for guessing what her verdict would be. He couldn't even use the mobile to ring

Patty Lake and let her know he wouldn't be coming. Dad always kept it on him, and after the row earlier, he wasn't going to ask Dad for any favours. He wasn't going to give him the chance to say "no".

Angrily Nicky scooped up a handful of loose gravel from the layer Mum had scattered by the trailer door. It was her attempt to try and protect the floor from the endless trail of muddy footprints every time it rained.

The stones made a light patter of sound as Nicky let them trickle through his fingers and rain back down into the grass.

Sky, their Alsatian, whimpered and sat beside him, pushing her nose anxiously into his lap. "You're supposed to be our guard dog. You're supposed to be tough and strong," Nicky whispered as he rubbed her ears absently. It was nice to have her there, to feel her warmth and her concern, but it wasn't really Sky he was thinking of. All his thoughts were turned towards that gawky skewbald horse at Mill Farm who was going to be put on trial tomorrow morning, and judged by a jury of two, who had already made up their minds.

He scratched up another handful of gravel, and this time flung it hard away from him, the stones shooting off like a tiny explosion into the evening.

6

It was gone four when Nicky managed to get out to Mill Farm.

The last ride was just leaving, the string of horses walking dutifully down the bridle track that led towards the woods.

Nicky stopped cycling and pulled his bike closer to the bushes to let them past. Lynette, who was leading on Blaze, pressed him suddenly into a trot. As she drew level with Nicky, she gave a quick swish with her crop, so that the chestnut started and bucked suddenly. She didn't look at Nicky, but Nicky couldn't miss seeing her thin, satisfied smile, just before Blaze cantered away.

He let the rest of the ride trot past, then wheeled his bike along the last bit of track and into the stable yard.

He heard Tom before he saw him. "Your cough's still bad. You didn't ought to be here."

"Lots to do on a weekend." Tom looked round from where he was sweeping leaves with an old broom, in a gap between the loose boxes.

Nicky was about to answer when he heard a friendly whicker, and a brown and white head nodded towards him over one of the stable doors. "Hey, mate." Nicky rested his bike against the five-barred gate that led into the field opposite, and walked over to rub Puzzle's nose. It was a relief to see he was still here. He turned back to Tom. "D'you know what happened this morning when Patty watched him?"

Tom put the broom down and walked over to Nicky. "I wasn't here. They did it before I arrived. Apparently Lynette rode him, and said it was worse than one of those nightmare fairground rides. She reckoned no kid would keep their balance on him. I came in for a bit of stick about buying him."

Nicky shut his eyes, pressing his forehead down on to Puzzle's nose. He'd known it would happen, but it was still hard to hear. "I'm sorry. You were only going on my word." He looked at Puzzle, now cheerfully chewing at the sleeve of his jacket. "So what's happening now?"

"She's contacted somebody. Some family that

wants a first pony for their daughter. They're coming over to look at him tomorrow."

Nicky pulled a face. He knew about families who just wanted "a first pony". It could be a five-minute wonder, ridden frantically for the first few months, and then stuck in a field and forgotten about when the next craze came along. He'd seen horses like that whose hooves got so long they curled and split at the edges. Horses that stood for weeks on end in fields of mud and nettles, often with no shelter from the sun or rain. Horses that grew thin and miserable through the long winter, when the family preferred to stay glued to the telly and the central heating, and the "first pony" was the last thing they could be bothered to brave the cold to check on.

Nicky knew he wasn't being fair, but as Puzzle nuzzled into his shoulder, he hated this unknown family who might be going to come and take this friendly, trusting little horse away.

"Tom, could you come up to the house with me a minute?" Nicky turned round as Patty Lake came over. Her hands kept twisting together, and she wouldn't look at Tom as she spoke. Nicky wondered what was up. She was always a bit scatty, but she looked more strung up than ever at the moment.

"Sure." Tom raised his eyebrows at Nicky, and walked stiffly after her. He was still coughing.

Nicky went into the tack room and got down one

of the grooming kits. It didn't make proper sense, but he was suddenly determined to make Puzzle smart. He couldn't stop him from being sold, but he could make him look good. He could try and stop the family from making jokes, or funny remarks, about their possible "first pony".

In the stable he worked hard, brushing the mottled coat until it shone. Puzzle loved the attention. He stood stock still as Nicky worked, his body giving little shivers of pleasure. His ears were pricked forward, and from time to time he turned to nudge at Nicky, making funny, friendly little grunts and snuffles. Suddenly, as Nicky began working round the front, Puzzle stretched his neck, pushed his nose against Nicky, and wrinkled back his front lips.

Nicky frowned. "What you up to, mate?"

Puzzle tossed his head, striking the ground suddenly with his front hoof, and bared his teeth again. "Hey! Pack it in. You won't do yourself any favours if you get a reputation as a horse that nips." Nicky raised his hand, about to push the horse's nose away, but Puzzle was too quick. His teeth snapped, his face rubbed against Nicky's fingers – and to Nicky's astonishment his mouth closed around the grooming brush Nicky had been working with.

He stood there with it in his teeth, sparks of mischief dancing in his dark eyes.

Nicky folded his arms and stepped back. "So what are you going to do with that?"

Puzzle tossed his head again, and took a pace nearer to Nicky. Then, with a funny, circular motion, he pressed the bristles against Nicky's arm and began to brush.

Nicky shook his head in amazement. He'd worked with all sorts of horses. Clever. Slow. Bossy. Nervous. It didn't matter what their problems were, at some point he always made sure he groomed them. It was what horses did to each other, and it was a way of making friends and gaining trust. But he'd never in his life met a horse who had wanted to groom him back like this. He laughed, rubbing his fingers down the funny white patch on Puzzle's face. "You're daft as a brush," he whispered. "What you going to do next? Pick out my feet?"

Outside Nicky heard the four o'clock ride come clattering back across the cobbled yard. Lynette was barking orders about feeding and un-tacking. In the drive near the house, cars came and went as parents arrived to take their children home.

Nicky took the brush gently from Puzzle's mouth and began working on him again, more determined than ever to make something special of this horse. Puzzle stood quietly now, leaning against Nicky as he worked, occasionally nudging his back, or his arm, and blowing contentedly.

28

The sun dipped lower, and birds began to swoop in flocks, heading towards the trees for the night. Nicky glanced out at the sky, then bent to work on Puzzle's legs, untangling the knots from his shaggy white fetlocks. He wondered where Tom had got to. They usually did the feeds about now.

"Ever heard the expression 'trying to make a silk purse out of a sow's ear'?"

Nicky was oiling Puzzle's hooves as Lynette appeared suddenly at the stable door. He didn't answer.

"It's an old country saying that means you can never make something plain and ugly look nice."

Nicky moved round to do the next hoof. "Ever heard the expression 'get lost'? It's an old Gypsy saying that means 'get lost'."

"I should watch what you say. You may not know who you're talking to."

"Unluckily for me, I know only too well. I could have done without knowing you, though."

"Well, it could be your lucky day. Your wish might be about to come true."

"What are you talking about?" Nicky did look up this time. Lynette's mouth was twisted into a half-smile and, even in the fading light, it was hard to miss the gleam of triumph in her eyes.

Just at that moment, Tom appeared behind her. Lynette's smile dropped off her face, and she turned away quickly. "Hi, Tom. Hope you're feeling better. I'm just going over to the office. There's a problem with the feed bill for this month."

She swung away, leaving Tom looking at Nicky over the stable door. He looked really old. Small. Shocked.

"What's up?" Nicky laid the oiling cloth on the edge of the feed trough. He'd been looking forward to showing Tom Puzzle's "trick", but this suddenly didn't seem to be a good time.

"She wants me to go." Tom broke into a spasm of coughing. When the coughing stopped, his eyes were watery bright.

"Go where?"

"Away. For ever. I'm being put out to grass."

Realization dawned slowly as Nicky walked over to Tom. "You mean you've been sacked?"

Tom shrugged. "Retired. Laid off. Call it what you like. She said she thought the job was too much for me. She's got all these plans for the future. She wants someone younger. Someone with a bit of energy..." His words trailed off, and it wasn't the cough this time which was choking his voice.

"How can she do that? You told me her dad was your friend. You even played together when you were boys. And you've worked here almost all your life. Straight from school."

"That's part of the problem. She thinks I've been

here too long. She wants what she called a 'new broom' sweeping the place."

"But no one knows horses like you do. She'll never find anyone to replace you…"

"Oh, Tom." Lynette re-appeared suddenly. "I'm just going up to the house. I've got a few things to discuss with Patty. I've mixed the feeds, but maybe you and Nicky could take them round. I really don't know how long I'm going to be."

Tom looked at Nicky, and Nicky looked at Tom.

"So that's it?" said Nicky at last, as Lynette's footsteps grew fainter. "*She's* the new broom?"

"Patty reckons Lynette's full of new ideas. She thinks she'll be able to turn the place round. And Lynette's good with other things too – things I've never really got to grips with. She can deal with the accounts, and all the business bits and pieces. She'll be like a proper manager."

"Oh Tom, I'm so sorry." Nicky spoke gently, and touched Tom's shoulder. "How long have you got left?"

"She wants me out straight away. I'm owed holiday time, so she said I can take that, rather than work out the month's notice."

Nicky shook his head, anger suddenly replacing the shock. "The witch!" he burst out suddenly. "Lynette's done all this. She's been plotting for it. Patty might think she's going to be a new broom, but as far as I can see, that's what Lynette should be riding round on."

Behind him, Puzzle nudged him gently in the back. Nicky turned round suddenly, and wound his arms round the horse's neck. He buried his head deep into the wiry mane, and kept it pressed hard for a moment as a fresh thought hit him. If Tom was going, that would be it for him as well. There was no way Lynette would want him around now that she was being a "proper manager".

His days at Mill Farm were over too.

7

"What d'you think of my new earrings?"

"They're a bit big." Nicky looked at Sabrina as she walked along beside him. "And girls aren't supposed to wear dangly ones at school."

"I'll take them off when the bell goes."

They walked in silence for a moment. Nicky was still running yesterday over in his mind. He'd hardly slept last night, worrying about how Tom was, worrying about what would happen to Puzzle, and worrying about where he could go to ride if Lynette told him to stay away. Perhaps if he just kept his head down, and did a good job, she'd keep him on. He could just about put up with her, for the sake of being around the horses.

"D'you think Mum will let me have a party for my birthday next week?"

Nicky tried to pull himself out of the heavy mood. "In the trailer?"

"I wouldn't be able to invite enough people there. I thought maybe I could have it at the 'Pig and Whistle'. They do them in there, in that side room. Kelly Lettings had hers there on Saturday."

Nicky looked carefully at his younger sister. She'd changed a lot since they'd moved here. She was small for her age, but she used to be tough with it. Now, she looked vulnerable. Fragile. When they lived with the others she was always full of fun. Racing around, getting into scrapes, being part of the gang. Now she looked like she wouldn't say "boo" to a goose.

"Have you got lots of mates at school then?" he said gently.

"I go round with Carla Jones and Kelly Lettings sometimes."

Nicky frowned. He knew Carla – her sister Tiff was in his class. She was one of those big-mouth girls, always in trouble but never seeming bothered about it. If Carla was anything like her sister – and from what Nicky had seen, she looked like she was – then Sabrina would do best to stay well clear of her. "What's Kelly like?" he asked carefully.

"She's a laugh." Sabrina's eyes brightened

suddenly. "She does mad things for a dare. Everyone likes her."

"I bet they do." Nicky's dry response was lost on his sister. "So how come you didn't go to her party on Saturday, if you're such good friends with her?"

"She was only allowed to ask ten friends, so she didn't have enough invitations for me. She said if anyone dropped out, she'd invite me then."

"Sounds like a great friend," Nicky muttered under his breath. He had a sudden urge to get hold of Sabrina and hug her really tight, like he used to when she was little.

They were nearing the school gates now, and without noticing it, both of them began dragging their feet, getting slower and slower. Other pupils were hurrying past them, calling and chattering. Cars drew up – mainly mums who were driving their children in from the new housing estates on the edge of town. They kept their engines running as the children scrambled out, and beeped their horns as they drove away.

"Hi, Sabrina. You coming in with us?" Kelly Lettings and Carla Jones appeared suddenly from across the road. Nicky looked them over. They both seemed tall next to Sabrina, and much older. They'd "adapted" their blue and white school uniforms to look like something from a fashion magazine, and Nicky noticed that Kelly was wearing lipstick.

He squeezed Sabrina's shoulder. "I'm going in now. I'm supposed to be getting the woodwork tools ready for a project this morning. I'll see you."

"See you." Sabrina gave him a vague smile. She stopped walking, and began fumbling in her bag for something.

As Nicky reached the gate, he glanced back.

Sabrina was hurrying to catch up with Carla and Kelly, who were wandering on ahead. They were walking close together, and laughing about something.

Nicky watched as Sabrina reached them, tugged at Kelly's elbow, then handed her something. It was a small parcel, wrapped in silver and gold striped paper. Nicky recognized the paper. It was the stuff Mum kept in the cupboard for wrapping up birthday presents.

8

"Country air. A fine, healthy smell." The man nodded vigorously, but his nose wrinkled slightly as he brushed at invisible hairs on his suit jacket.

The woman tottered beside him, stopping occasionally to pick off the pats of mud and straw that kept collecting on her high heels. She smiled brightly at Nicky. "We've got a dinner party after this. I wasn't going to have time to change."

Nicky nodded briefly, but his eyes were on the girl trudging sulkily behind them – the one that Puzzle was meant for. She looked about Sabrina's age. She was very thin. Colourless skin. Light brown hair cut round very straight, and hanging just below her shoulders. She was wearing a baggy white T-shirt that almost drowned her, and ankle socks with sandals under a long flowery skirt. Unless she was planning to go side-saddle, she obviously wasn't intending to ride.

"Of course, Jade knows all about horses. She's had lessons since she was four. We would have got her a pony before, but the stables were such a drive away, and I don't have much time to keep ferrying her about. There's a paddock just behind our new house, so it's not a problem any more." The woman flashed a smile at Nicky, her even white teeth showing lipstick stains which were a perfect match for her bright pink jacket. Her tone changed suddenly. "Max! Come here!" She turned towards a stocky red-headed boy of about six, who was doing a tightrope walk along the outside trough. Max jumped down and began weaving his way down the yard, his arms stretched out like an aeroplane.

"Boys, eh?" The woman laughed brightly. "What can you do with them?"

Patty came hurrying over, her hand outstretched. "Mr and Mrs Snedworth. I'm so pleased to see you. I hope you didn't have any trouble finding us."

Mr Snedworth laughed loudly. "With my wife navigating, it was lucky we didn't end up in the wilds of Scotland."

Patty turned to Nicky. "Can you get Puzzle for us, please?"

Nicky unlatched the door, and Puzzle followed him out quietly, stopping when Nicky stopped, in front of the family.

Patty smiled round at them all. "See, he's very gentle. He's perfect for a first pony."

Max squirmed down from the gate he was hanging upside-down on, ran up and poked Puzzle in the belly.

"Keep away from his legs, dear." Mrs Snedworth made a grab for Max's elbow, but he twisted away from her and ran off towards the hose pipe.

Mr Snedworth walked over and slapped Puzzle hard on the neck. "Seems like a solid piece of meat. What d'you think, dear?"

Mrs Snedworth made a clicking noise with her tongue, and turned to Jade. "I know you really had your heart set on a white one, like Vicki's got…"

"Grey." Jade kicked a stone as she spoke, and didn't even look at Puzzle. "White horses are never called white. They're called grey."

"Is that true? Well, I didn't know that. You learn something new every day, don't you?" Mrs Snedworth nudged Jade, then gave a shrill laugh, as if she'd cracked a joke.

Jade just shrugged.

Patty chewed her thumbnail and forced a smile at Jade. "Is he for you?"

"Apparently."

"Perhaps you'd like to walk round with him a bit. See how you feel then."

Jade shrugged again. "I don't like the look of him. He looks like he's been crossed with a cow."

"Jade!" Mrs Snedworth twittered nervously as she turned to Patty. "We're really just looking at the moment. This is the first one we've seen."

At that moment Lynette appeared, walking out from the tack room. "You're the family who've come to see Puzzle, are you?" She smiled brightly, letting her eyes run over Jade for a moment. "It's such a shame none of you have come dressed for riding. Still, I'm sure Nicky could take him round for us, just to put him through his paces. It was Nicky who chose him for us in the first place, and he knows lots about horses. He's a lovely ride, isn't he, Nicky?"

She handed the tack to Nicky, and stood back to watch as he got Puzzle ready.

"See – gentle as a lamb." She smiled round at Mr Snedworth, who was rubbing at his shoe with a handkerchief.

Mr Snedworth straightened up, folded the handkerchief neatly, and put it in his jacket pocket. "Well, we're not…" He stopped short as Puzzle suddenly stretched out his neck, wrinkled back his top lip, then very gently pulled the handkerchief back out. "Hey!"

"He's a bit of a comedian." Lynette shot a daggered look at Nicky, then smiled brightly at Mr Snedworth again. "He's got loads of character. He's a really 'fun' horse…"

"Jade's an excellent rider. We want her to have a horse that challenges her skills," Mrs Snedworth interrupted hurriedly. "Her last instructor said she's more than ready to start competing in shows this summer." She gave a short, girlish giggle, and nudged Jade again.

Jade stared away into the distance, and didn't answer.

Lynette gave a sharp tug on the handkerchief, and there was a tiny ripping sound as Puzzle jerked his head sideways before dropping it on to the cobbles. Lynette handed it back to Mr Snedworth. Her smile was beginning to dazzle. "I'm sure Puzzle can rise to meet any need. That's the joy of having something so willing. And of course – " she glanced across at Max, who was firing a toy water pistol at Muffet, the ginger stable cat – "there's a great benefit in your getting an animal that all the family could make use of."

Mrs Snedworth shuddered and laughed loudly. "Oh, you don't mean me, do you? I'm more of a tennis fanatic myself. And Nigel has his golf. We really wouldn't have time…"

"Well, see what you think." Lynette's voice was

still sugar-sweet, but the smile had melted. "There's no pressure to make up your mind today of course – only I do have someone else coming to see him later. Are you ready, Nicky?"

Nicky nodded, swung into the saddle and rode Puzzle across the yard to the field. Puzzle walked willingly, not even flinching as Max came swooping up behind them, shouting, "Watch out! The space shuttle is about to crash!"

Puzzle was even more uncomfortable to ride this time. The saddle seemed to go against his movements, as if it was fighting to follow a different rhythm altogether. It took Nicky a moment to get the feel of it, and all his skill to make it look easy. But once he'd relaxed into it, he managed to trot, then canter through perfect figures of eight before stopping suddenly, with Puzzle standing square and still as a statue. Nicky could tell that, for all his funny looks, this horse had been trained well in the beginning. He was giving everything he'd got, and he was as solid and reliable as a rock.

He glanced towards the gate, wondering what sort of reaction they were getting.

Mr Snedworth was peering into the wing mirror of the horse-box, straightening his tie.

Mrs Snedworth had got Max by the shoulder, and was pointing a finger at him. Max was screaming back at her, using a string of words

Nicky guessed she would have preferred him not to know.

Jade was trudging slowly back up towards the car.

Only Patty and Lynette were still leaning on the gate, and something about the way they were watching told Nicky they weren't going to be presenting him with a silver horseshoe when he rode back out.

Angrily, Nicky pushed Puzzle into a slow canter, letting him stretch his neck out and move freely. As far as Nicky was concerned, the whole family could get stuffed. It would have been a disaster if Puzzle had ended up with a rabble like that anyway.

Just in front of him was a low jump, a red-and-white striped pole about half a metre off the ground. Trying to burn off his black mood, Nicky turned Puzzle towards it. Immediately Puzzle went slower, twisting his body slightly and cantering sideways. Nicky tried to straighten him out, pulling his head round and urging him forwards with his legs. Puzzle seemed to twist even further and slowed to a strange, rocking sort of trot. Nicky cursed under his breath. That was all he needed – for Patty and Lynette to watch Puzzle refuse a jump. He could end up as dog food if he wasn't careful.

As they reached the jump Puzzle stopped completely, gave a tiny half buck, and then leapt over. It was so clumsy – and it was such a surprise – that, for the first time in years, Nicky felt himself rise out of the saddle, hang for a moment around Puzzle's neck, then slide in an undignified heap to the ground.

9

Puzzle stopped, turned, and trotted back towards Nicky. He pushed his nose against his shoulder, snorting anxiously.

"I was trying to do you a favour." Nicky stood up slowly, dusting himself down. "You don't know how to help yourself."

Puzzle nuzzled him again.

Nicky sighed. "You've made a right fool of me. Especially with those two watching."

Puzzle's head drooped slightly, and he looked away.

"OK, I know. You're sorry." Nicky picked up the reins, and stared hard into Puzzle's eyes. "We'll do it again. Just so we don't end on a bad note. But don't mess me about this time."

He swung into the saddle, leaning back slightly to keep Puzzle on course as they cantered towards the jump. It didn't work. It was the same as before. Puzzle twisted sideways, slowed and almost stopped, bucked, then lurched over the pole.

At least this time Nicky was ready. At least this time he didn't fall. "We'll do it again. We'll sort this out," he muttered, pulling Puzzle round.

There was no difference.

"You stubborn old mule. I'll make it higher. You'll *have* to go over straight then." Nicky was frustrated – with Puzzle and with himself. It wasn't just about proving anything to Patty and Lynette any more. Nicky knew horses. He knew how to make them listen to him. He knew how to make them do exactly what he wanted. Now, for the first time ever, he'd met a horse who was determined to do things his own way, even if it made them both look stupid.

Nicky raised the pole, and raised the pole, and raised the pole. Each time Puzzle jumped it with the same funny sideways buck, stop, and leap.

Nicky was suddenly aware of people coming across the field towards him. It was Patty, Lynette, and a girl with red hair that he'd never seen before.

Lynette and Patty were hanging back, talking quietly with their heads close together. The girl broke away from them and came towards Nicky, smiling. "Hi. I'm Megan Wise. I got a message at the yard where I work that you had a horse for sale, so I've come to have a look." She put her hand up to stroke Puzzle's nose, and he nudged her gently. "I thought he was amazing just now. I've never seen anything like it before."

"What d'you mean?"

"The way he jumps. Look at the height he cleared. He's wonderful."

For the first time, Nicky took a proper look at the poles. They were well over a metre and a half high now – as tough as anything that even Blaze could manage, and that was with months of training. He'd been so busy trying to get Puzzle to jump straight, he hadn't noticed how much he'd raised them. "He's strong as an ox. Once he'd made his mind up about which way he was going, I didn't stand a chance."

Megan ran her fingers through Puzzle's mane. "It's great to see a horse with a mind of his own. I know he's got an odd action, but there's loads of potential. If I could manage to stay on, he might be just want I'm looking for."

Nicky smiled suddenly. He liked Megan. He liked her warm, round face, and her friendly smile. If Puzzle had to go anywhere, she would give him a great home.

He jumped off, and handed the reins to her. "D'you want to try him yourself?"

Patty and Lynette came up as Megan put her foot in the stirrup.

"I'm afraid there's not much point you riding him," Lynette's eyes were small, and hard, and glittery bright. "I'm really sorry we've wasted your time, but there's been a mistake. This horse isn't for sale after all."

Megan's face clouded with disappointment. "That's a shame. I was very interested in him. I really thought he could do well."

Lynette took Puzzle's reins from her, and Megan gave them all a brief nod, and walked back across the field.

"What's going on?" Nicky frowned. "I thought you couldn't wait to get rid of him."

"Change of plan," Lynette said crisply. "Oh – and by the way – I can manage him on my own. I won't be needing you over here any more." Then she looped Puzzle's reins over his head, and led him away towards the stables.

10

"What was she doing here?" Nicky leant his bike against the side of Tom's bungalow, and watched as Lynette kicked Blaze into a canter, and rode off towards the woods behind the water mill.

"A bit of a chat." Tom's voice was guarded. Nicky pulled an old station bench round into the shade of an ancient apple tree, and Tom lowered himself on to it.

"I bet you were delighted to see her." Nicky went to the corrugated iron shed where Tom kept his tools, and took down a pair of gardening shears. They were spotted with rust, and when he tried to open them they were jammed solid. He rummaged to find oil and rags, and a metal file, and went back to kneel beside the bench. Maggie waddled over and began cleaning her feathers in the long grass by Tom's feet.

Tom watched Nicky. "You don't need to do that."

"I want to." Nicky rubbed hard at the crusty old metal. "Anyway, it keeps my mind off things."

"What sort of things?"

"Her for a start." He jerked his head in the direction Lynette had taken. He worked in silence for a moment, and then added, "You know she told me yesterday I had to leave, don't you? That they wouldn't be needing me at Mill Farm any more?"

Tom sighed. "I guessed she might come out with something like that. She wouldn't want you taking all the glory."

"What d'you mean?"

"With the horse. Puzzle. If he jumps as well as you told me, she'll have plans for him. And she'll want to do them on her own."

"What sort of plans?" Nicky tried cutting the air with the shears. They creaked a ragged protest, but they opened slowly.

"She'll be competing him, most likely. She'll be wanting to make a name for herself through the horse."

"But she can't stand even to look at him. Some of the things she said—"

"That won't matter to Lynette any more. She's

ambitious. She's a girl that plans ahead, and right now it seems to her that Puzzle might be able to give her something she wants. If he doesn't ... well, she'll just drop him again."

Nicky stood up and began hacking at the grass round the legs of the bench.

Maggie watched him warily, but she didn't move. "So he's just a tool to get her what she wants?"

Tom twisted round to look at Nicky, coughing slightly with the effort. "Don't be too hard on her. She's hungry to be special – to get herself noticed. She's just seen her chance through that horse."

Nicky snapped the shears angrily. "Why do you have to be so ... so *nice* all the time? You lost your job because of her."

Tom slumped against the back of the bench again, and shook his head. "That's not really true. I lost my job because I got old, and sick. Lynette didn't make any of that happen."

"She was hovering though – like a vulture waiting to pick at your bones."

Tom gave a dry laugh, which finished in a spasm of coughing. "Hang on. I'm not dead. I'm only retired. It happens to most people, you know."

"Sorry." Nicky stopped cutting, and straightened up to look at Tom. The couple of days' rest didn't seem to be making him look any better. "So what did she want, anyway?"

A shadow darkened Tom's eyes, and he looked away. "She came to make me an offer…"

"What sort of an offer?"

"About this place."

"She just won't leave off, will she? What's this place got to do with her?"

"Quite a lot, I'm afraid. Or at least, it's got a lot to do with Patty."

"Go on."

Tom turned his troubled eyes to Nicky. "I know everyone thinks of it as mine. I think of it like that too. I seem to have lived here for ever. But the truth is, I've never actually owned this bungalow…"

Nicky let the shears drop with a clatter, making Maggie flap her good wing and hiss suddenly. "So who does?"

"The land has been in Patty's family for years. The mill was theirs too – it was her grandfather who was running it at the time it closed down. This bungalow went with my job. Now that I'm not working for her…" Tom broke off into another fit of coughing.

"But she can't just chuck you out. There's laws and things."

"She could make it difficult if she wanted to. She's got plans…"

Nicky suddenly remembered the man with the dark suit and the notebook. "She wants to develop it?"

"It's not definite…"

"But you could still stay here," Nicky insisted. "They can't make you go."

Tom ran his eye all round the bungalow, and the garden, and the fields beyond.

Nearby, butterflies danced between tangled wild flowers. The fields shimmered emerald green. Over by the water mill a breeze swayed the tips of the tallest reeds, and in the bright June light even the mill itself seemed touched with gold.

"Imagine it, Nicky," he said at last. "All this gone. Neat boxes of houses everywhere. Smart cars and postage-stamp gardens, and everybody watching everybody else from out of their windows. And then, squashed between it all, would be me – a funny, quirky old man in a bungalow that's falling to bits. They'd be kind enough, I'm sure – but we'd all know they were just waiting for me to go. All the time I'm here, I'll be keeping their house prices down." Tom shook his head slowly. Maggie stretched her neck, then rested her beak on his knee. "I don't reckon I'd want to live like that. I don't reckon I'd want to die like that either."

For a long time neither of them spoke.

Then, putting his hand briefly on Tom's thin shoulder, Nicky squeezed him gently. "I don't reckon I'd want that for you either," he said.

Bending down, he picked up the shears again,

and began cutting the grass, until the rough wooden handles rubbed blisters into his skin.

Tom fell asleep with Maggie's head still in his lap, snoring raggedly under the brilliant blue of the summer sky.

11

"Where's Mum and Dad?"

"Out shopping. Jim's outside."

"I know. I saw him just now when I was coming in. Hey … that's good. What's it for?" Nicky leaned over Sabrina's shoulder to watch as she as she carefully wove brown felt-tip patterns into a drawing of a scrawny brown duckling.

"It's for that poster competition. You know – on *Crazy About Creatures*."

"Are you going to enter it then?"

"I don't know yet. Miss Anderson at school's gone potty about the whole thing. We have to do a class collection of postcards, and this poster is for homework. She's going to enter any that are good enough."

"There can't be many others in your class who could draw better ducks than that."

Sabrina wrinkled her nose and shrugged. "It doesn't have to be a duck. It could be any sort of wild animal. Kelly and Carla are doing one together, and they've done a fox in a dustbin. It looks really good."

Nicky helped himself to an apple from the fruit bowl, and took a bite. "Sounds like cheating."

"Not really. They're just good friends. They always do everything together."

Nicky took another bite from the apple, and flopped back along the seat. Closing his eyes, pictures immediately swamped his head of Tom, and the bungalow, the sudden, brutal image of bulldozers and diggers and men in hard hats.

"Oh, by the way – that Lynette was here earlier."

Nicky's eyes flew open. "What did she want?"

"Don't know. She only stayed about five minutes, and she spoke to Dad outside."

"I expect she was telling Dad she sent me packing from Mill Farm yesterday."

Sabrina squinted at her picture for a moment, then looked up. "Whatever it was, Dad was smiling when he came back in."

"He would be!" Suddenly angry, Nicky aimed the unfinished apple at the bin, and flung it. It missed, and hit the cabinet behind with a heavy *thwack*. Bits of the soft fruit squelched out, making

56

a juicy stain on the woodwork.

"You'd better clean that up before Mum gets back. A wasted apple *and* a squidgy mess on that door won't get you any prizes."

Nicky pulled a floor cloth from the cupboard under the sink, and wiped the stain angrily. Trust Dad to be pleased that he wasn't going to be able to be around horses. And trust Lynette to be the one creeping about, telling him. She was like poison ivy. The only good thing about leaving Mill Farm was that he was going to be able to keep away from her, except this was already the second time today she'd seeped into his life.

"What do you think?" Sabrina held up the finished duck picture.

Nicky shook the splatterings of apple out of the cloth and into the bin, then forced himself to look interested. "It's great," he nodded. "Really special." He suddenly meant it too. It wasn't just the colours, and the shapes, and the delicate details on the wings and face. The whole picture had a warmth about it, as if the funny, fuzzy-headed little duck might waddle out of the paper at any minute. "That duck could break people's hearts."

"That was what I wanted you to say." Sabrina grinned and pushed a strand of hair back behind her ears. "Now all I've got to do is the writing. How do you spell 'environment'?"

"E – N – V – " Nicky stopped. "Oh, I don't know. Look it up in the dictionary."

Sabrina blushed. "Will you do it for me? I never quite get how they work."

"Have you got one then?"

"No."

"Well, neither have I. You'll just have to try and guess it." Nicky was secretly relieved that he wouldn't have to wade through pages and pages of words, looking for something he might not be able to find.

He was about to get himself a can of coke from the fridge, when a knock at the door rattled the trailer. He glanced at Sabrina, who had her head down, concentrating on the poster again.

"You get that," she muttered. "It's probably that Lynette coming back."

"It'd better not be." Nicky hesitated.

The door rattled again.

"OK, OK." Angrily he put the coke back in the fridge, went to the door, and flung it open.

"Is Sabrina in?" Kelly and Carla stood there, dressed as if they were off to a disco, giggling and nudging at each other.

Before Nicky had a chance to answer, Sabrina appeared behind him. "Hi … I didn't expect…"

"We were just passing." Kelly glanced at Nicky and giggled again. "Can we come in?"

Nicky stepped aside and Sabrina led them through into the trailer.

"Isn't it sweet." Carla stood in the middle by the cooker, looking round at everything. "My dad's got a kitchen a bit like this in his house. He likes it 'cause he can still watch telly when he's doing the cooking. His is much bigger, of course. How many of you are there?"

"There's five of us altogether."

"Don't forget the monkey," Nicky muttered.

"Have you got a monkey? How sweet."

"Don't take any notice of him; he's in a funny mood." Sabrina pulled a face at Nicky. "Do you want a coke?"

"OK." Carla and Kelly giggled some more, fussing with their skirts and giving odd little looks at Nicky as they wriggled themselves down on to the seat.

Kelly turned back to Sabrina. "So where do you sleep?"

"On hammocks. Outside." Nicky fixed his eyes on hers. "So we can gaze at the stars."

"Really?" Her eyes widened. "What happens when it rains?"

"We get wet."

"Stop it, Nicky." Sabrina walked across with the cokes. "Honestly, we sleep on beds just like everybody else. These seats fold out at night time for us. Mum and Dad sleep on the other side of the trailer, with the screen down, and I sleep over here."

"And what about Nicky?" Carla shot Kelly a glance, and they both giggled again.

"Next door, with Jim. He's Dad's older cousin and—"

"Hey – that's good." Kelly interrupted her, and leaned across to the table to look at Sabrina's poster.

"That's my homework. For that competition."

"It's really sweet." Carla wriggled forward to take a closer look, twisting back the ring pull on her coke can as she leaned across. The frothy brown liquid fizzed up suddenly, bubbling over the top, then exploded down on to the paper, smearing the patterns of the brown and black feathers. "Oh, sorry…"

"Don't worry. I'll sort it out." Sabrina grabbed the cloth that Nicky had left on the side earlier, and began frantically dabbing at the paper. She rubbed gently, but it was no good. The feathers were now a smudged blotchy stain, and the colours on the face had run so that the bright beautiful eyes now spread like long dark tears.

"Good job it was only a practice one." Carla licked a trickle of coke off the back of her hand.

"It…" Sabrina looked up at her, her eyes glistening suddenly.

"It was, wasn't it?" Kelly cut in. "I mean, you couldn't have entered it like that, could you?"

"I…"

"Course she couldn't." Carla wiped her fingers on the back of the seats. "I mean, you'd have to spell 'environment' right first, wouldn't you?"

"Course it was only a practice." Nicky, who had been watching quietly, butted in suddenly. "She just did that one really quickly. She can draw a zillion times better than that when she really works at something."

Sabrina gave him a wobbly smile. "Course I can," she said brightly. "If I can be bothered." She turned back to the others. "D'you want to watch some telly?"

Carla took a sip of coke, and turned to Sabrina. "Could do."

"We'll need to check in the crystal ball first, to see what's on." The hard edge in Nicky's voice was lost on Kelly and Carla, and he shrugged suddenly. "I'm going out. Are you going to be OK?"

"Why shouldn't I be?" Sabrina grabbed the brown duck poster, scrumpled it up into a soggy, tight ball, and chucked it across the trailer. It hit the cabinet on the same spot as the apple had, then rolled down to rest against the bin. She didn't go and pick it up. Instead, she grabbed the remote control, and began to flick through the channels.

12

Outside, Jim was working on a fresh load of logs.

Nicky walked over to him. "I'll give you a hand with that."

Jim stopped, his leathered brown face beaded with sweat. "Maybe for ten minutes then." He handed Nicky the small axe. "Just to give my hands a bit of a rest."

Nicky got started, lopping off the thin leafy twigs that sprouted all along the chopped branches. Jim sat beside him, rubbing at his fingers, kneading his swollen knuckles and joints. For a while, neither of them spoke.

"Your mum and dad are back." Jim watched the pick-up bounce across the grass and roll to a stop near the trailers. "Your mum will be cooking soon. I'll take some of these smaller branches and build a fire ready for the evening, for after we've eaten."

Nicky glanced across, but didn't stop working as Mum struggled to lift a box of groceries from the back of the pick-up, and carried it inside.

"Got some good work coming up." Dad walked over to Nicky, and stood watching him.

Nicky was using the bow-saw, cutting the trimmed branches into equal lengths. "Like what?"

"That Annie Hobbs. She was pleased with the job your mum and I did the other day, and she said there should be more coming in soon."

"More what?" Nicky began to stack the branches into a neat pile as he cut them.

"Old furniture mainly. She's trying to build up that side of her business – doing up tables and wardrobes and stuff like that. It could be the beginning."

"What of?"

"Getting regular work at last. If we're gaining a reputation of being honest, reliable and reasonably priced, the word will get round soon enough."

"Great." Nicky gave Dad a brief nod. It was good news, after all. Dad had been battling to get a good name for himself ever since they'd settled here, but some gorgios were against them without ever meeting them – just because they were

Gypsies. It wasn't anything new. They'd met all sorts of prejudices when they were travelling, but Dad wanted them to make a permanent home here now, and having to stay in one place made it harder to live with.

Nicky wiped the sweat off his forehead with the back of his hand, and shifted position. For a while there was no sound but the rasping grate of the saw.

"Oh – and something else. Someone you know came over. That girl from Mill Farm."

Nicky finished the last branch, and rooted about in Jim's bag for the big splitting axe. "Sabrina told me. I suppose she was moaning about me."

"No, she wasn't. She came with the offer of some work. Annie Hobbs put in a word for us. Told her we were good with odd jobs in woodwork and stuff."

Nicky picked the top log back off the pile. He positioned it on a stub of sawn-off trunk that had come from an oak tree they had felled once. They used it as a kind of cutting table. As he raised the axe, he tried to imagine what "odd jobs" Lynette might have in mind for Dad at Mill Farm. Some of the stable doors needed sorting out, and the fences needed repairing, but there wasn't much. Tom may not have been the "proper manager" Patty Lake had suddenly decided she needed, but he'd kept the place together. They'd notice a difference now – unless Lynette brought in cheap labour from someone like Dad. He let the axe drop, splitting the branch into two halves. "You won't need work like that. They won't want to pay you much, for a start."

Dad laughed. "Well, they'll pay me a bit more than they ever paid you, that's for sure. And I'm not in a position to turn work away from anyone."

"But they're a miserable pair. Especially Lynette."

"It's never bothered you. You'd be over there every spare minute if I let you."

"Not any more. I don't go there now."

"Well, that's news to me. And anyway, if we do get offered some work from her, I'll need you with me."

"Oh, great!" Nicky positioned the split branch again, this time splintering it into quarters. That was all he needed, having to go over there as the "odd job" boy. It was bad enough not being able to work with the horses, but it would be torture to have to walk past Puzzle and the others as if they meant nothing to him. Lynette knew what she was doing. She was really rubbing his nose in it. He'd be like a street kid with his face pressed up against a toy shop window.

He reached for another branch.

Dad took the split logs and laid them down, starting up a new stack. "She was making me a fair offer of work. Not just at the stables, but other places as well."

"What d'you mean, other places? She's only the head groom there. She's not lady of the manor."

"No, but that Lake woman she works for is, and that was what she was suggesting for me."

"I don't get you."

"There's other work coming up. Land clearance over by the old water mill, for instance."

Nicky sliced the axe hard into the log, flakes of bark flying up in the air. "No, Dad. You can't. Not there. It's Tom's place. It's his home."

"Lynette told me he'd be leaving soon. Patty Lake's offered him a flat in town."

The words cut through Nicky. A flat in town. *A flat in town!* He raised the axe again, but his hand was shaking suddenly, and he didn't trust himself to aim straight. "She can't." He turned to Dad. "She couldn't. It will kill him."

"From what she was telling me this afternoon, it'll kill him if he doesn't go."

"But Tom's like us. He's used to fields, and countryside, and open spaces. He'll hate it."

"He'll get used to it. We all have to get used to change. It's just the way the world moves round." Dad's eyes met and held Nicky's, then he turned and stalked off into the trailer.

Nicky let the branch he was holding fall to the

ground. Then he swung the axe again, feeling the impact shake through him as it hit a giant blow into the felled oak stub. He left it there, the blade wedged deep in the wood. Then he turned, kicking at the stacks of logs. The top ones wobbled, then toppled slowly down. Unbalanced, the others followed, sliding into an untidy sprawl across the grass. Nicky stared at them for a moment, and then turned and walked away.

13

"I want you to start on the stables at the bottom. Some of the wood's beginning to rot, and I need it sorted while the weather's fine." Lynette was brisk as Dad and Nicky followed her down the yard. Nicky kept his eyes fixed straight ahead, trying to ignore the soft whicker and whinny of the horses who tossed their heads in greeting as he walked by.

Puzzle's stable was empty. It was three days since Nicky had last seen him, and he felt a wrench in his chest, wondering where he was. He wasn't going to ask, anyway.

"OK then, I'll leave you to it. I'm assuming you both know what you're doing, and Patty's waiting in the field for me." Nicky could feel Lynette's eyes watching him as she spoke. He bent down to unzip the tool bag, and refused to look back at her.

They got busy as soon as she left, Nicky sanding off the old paintwork, and Dad setting in repairs and replacement planks.

Nicky fixed his mind on the job. There was a kind of comfort, almost a soothing, that came from the endless methodical rubbing and scraping.

"You look hot. I brought some cokes in the bag. Do you want one now?"

"No, thanks." It was a warm evening, and Nicky was sweltering. The sanding had peppered his hair and face, making them ash grey. His throat felt dry as dust. But he didn't want to stop. He didn't want to relax. He didn't want to be stuck here for a second longer than he had to be.

"That's looking good." Patty Lake appeared from round the corner. "It's going to make a real difference."

"It'll take a bit of time, but once it's done the wood will stay sound for years." Dad got up from the pile of planks he'd been resting on, and shook her hand.

"Sounds great. Just what I need." Patty sighed, then turned to Nicky. "Before you go, could you come up to the house? There's something I need to talk to you about."

"He can come now if you want."

Nicky shot Dad a look of disgust.

Dad weakened, reading Nicky's thoughts. "Maybe there's somewhere else you could talk to him? Our family gets a bit strange about being in houses."

"I see." Patty chewed a loose scratch of skin on the edge of her finger. "Would you be happier in one of the stables?"

"No. It's OK." Nicky stood up, suddenly not wanting to be shut in a stable with her either, with all those familiar smells and feelings drenching him on all sides. He gave her a thin smile. "I'll give your house a try."

"Good lad." Dad clapped him hard on the back. "You can't go on hiding from stuff like that for ever. You both go on up, and I'll finish off here. I'm sure I can manage on my own."

Silently Nicky followed Patty back up the yard, along the wide gravel drive, and up to the house. It was an old place, made of flint. The windows were leaded lights, and very small. They looked to Nicky as if they would shut out the sun. He had never been this close before, and he could see that some of the tiny diamond panes were cracked. A couple were completely missing. It surprised him. He hadn't realized it was so shabby.

They walked past Patty's ancient blue car – the words "Clean Me" scrawled across the dusty bonnet – and on to the front door. Patty glanced back at Nicky as she pushed on it. "Will it help if I leave it open?"

Nicky looked through at the thin, dark hallway. Already his heart was pounding. "It might do." Taking a deep breath, he followed Patty into the kitchen.

"Sit down." Patty moved a pile of newspapers off one of the chairs, and pulled out a seat round a huge pine table. "Excuse the mess. I just never seem to have time…"

Nicky sat, still breathing deeply, as she hurriedly cleared away breakfast cereals, a carton of milk, and a cracked dirty mug. The room smelt stuffy and dank, and it was a relief when she opened the window over the sink.

An ancient yellow Labrador heaved itself up from a pile of rugs, and waddled over to sniff his legs. "I didn't know you had a dog." Nicky bent to stroke it. An animal was a good thing to focus on.

"Meet Brutus," Patty smiled. "He's completely blind, and about a hundred and ten, in dog years. He used to belong to my father." Patty waved a hand at a fly that was buzzing round an open tin of beans. It flew off, but soon found its way back. Nicky saw it crawl about on the lid for a moment, and then disappear inside.

"Do you want a drink? I'm dangerously in need

of coffee." Patty filled the kettle, and began rinsing mugs out while it boiled.

"Er ... no, thanks." Nicky ruffled Brutus's ears, racking his brain for something to say. "Did your dad always live here?"

"He was born here, same as me. It's a family home. Goes back generations." Patty came and sat opposite him at the table. "The fields used to be farm land, growing wheat for the mill. After the mill closed, Grandfather kept the crops going, but they were hard years and it never really paid. After he died my father built the stables himself. It was a dream of his, to have a really successful stables – something new that did well, instead of old stuff that kept failing."

"That sounds really good – to have built a place up, and live your own dream."

Patty shook her head. "It never happened. It was always a struggle. I didn't realize quite how much, until my father died, and I got stuck with all the bills – and the debts. This place has never paid for itself either."

"Will you have to sell up then?"

"Oh no. I'd die before I let my father's dream fade away. I'm determined to make this place work, whatever it takes. Which brings me to my point." The faraway look that had softened Patty's usually tense expression disappeared. "I want to ask you a

72

favour. In fact, it's a bit more than a favour – it's a request."

"Go on." Nicky looked down at Brutus and twisted his collar between his fingers. She must be about to ask him and Dad to do the place up cheap.

"It's about Puzzle."

Nicky's head jerked up again. "What about him?"

"Well," Patty spoke slowly, weighing her words, "I don't know if you're aware of it, but Lynette's got high hopes for him."

"She's changed her tune."

"She recognizes potential when she sees it. There's nothing wrong with that. If my father could've managed to think like that a bit more, I might not be in the mess I'm in now."

Nicky didn't answer, and after a moment Patty went on, "She can see a bright future with that horse, but she's got a problem."

"What's that?"

"Well – this isn't Lynette's version of the story, but it's what I think is probably closest to the truth – she just can't manage him when he jumps. I haven't seen her fall off, but he unbalances her every time. She can't get used to his action."

"And what's her version?"

Patty smiled. "That she's too busy. And I think we'll have to let her think we believe that. You know how proud she is."

Nicky was about to say that he thought pride was the least of Lynette's faults, but he bit back the words.

"Anyway, I'm sure you can see it would be a disaster if she rode him in competitions, and then actually fell off. It would make Mill Farm look worse, and not better."

"It would make a right fool of her too."

"Well, yes. Only of course she hasn't said that."

"I don't expect she has." Nicky tried to keep the edge of irritation out of his voice. "But if you're asking me to work with Puzzle, and try to 'cure' him, I'd be leading you up the garden path. He's a great little horse, but I've never met an animal so stubborn before. He does things his own way, and I don't think anyone could change him."

"I didn't exactly want you to change him…"

"But you want me to train with him?" Nicky was torn between the thought of being allowed back with Puzzle again, and the knowledge that he couldn't really do anything to help. "However much I practise on him here, Lynette's still going to have to risk making a fool of herself on the big day each time."

"Not necessarily…"

"Well, it's not much good training him if nobody can ride him."

"But *you* can ride him." Patty spoke softly. "You

74

can train him, and then compete on him. In fact, we want you to compete in the next local gymkhana for us."

"A *gymkhana*!" Nicky made it sound like a swear word as he stood up suddenly, shaking the table, slopping Patty's coffee, and making Brutus slope anxiously back to his rugs. "You want *me* to enter a gymkhana?"

Patty looked confused. "It's quite normal—"

"Not for me it isn't. It'll be full of gorgios – non-gypsies – dressed in poncy jackets and talking in posh voices. We don't *do* gymkhanas. Even Dad wouldn't put me through a thing like that!"

There was a long silence, then Patty said in a small voice, "But you're the only one who's going to be able to stay on him. And you're the one who's going to be able to get the best out of him while you're doing it."

Nicky shook his head. "I'm sorry. You're asking too much. I'll help you out. I'll ride him for you, and try and get rid of some of those funny habits, but there's no way you'll ever get me into a gymkhana with him, or any other horse."

Patty spread her hands out in front of her in a hopeless gesture, and sighed. "I'm sorry. I didn't mean to offend you. I was just ... desperate."

"You'll have to sell him on then. There must be someone else who could manage him." Nicky suddenly remembered something. "That girl was interested – Megan something or other. The one who came over when I was jumping him on Sunday. Why don't you contact her?"

"You don't understand. I don't *want* to sell Puzzle. Lynette thinks he could turn things round for us here, if he starts winning prizes. We'll get good publicity. Our name will spread. More people will come here." Her voice was suddenly pleading, "Look around you. I'm only just about keeping things ticking over as it is."

Nicky walked across to the kitchen window. Out in the garden there were weeds everywhere, and the grass was already too long. Tom might have let his own place go, but he'd struggled hard to keep everything tidy round here. It was one of his "end of the day" jobs, but Nicky guessed Lynette wouldn't have got that written into her job description.

Thinking about Tom, a thought suddenly struck him, shuddering through him like a jolt from an axe.

He turned slowly, looking back at Patty. "Supposing I said yes. Supposing I agreed. There'd have to be some sort of a deal."

Patty met his gaze. "Name your price."

"Tom." Nicky said quietly.

Patty shook her head. "I'd do anything but that,

Nicky. I really can't take him back. He's just not up to it. It's for his own good, as well as mine…"

"I'm not talking about you taking him back. That wasn't what I meant."

"What then?"

"I want you to stop the development. I want you to leave Tom in peace."

Once again, Patty shook her head. "Now *you're* asking too much, Nicky. That land is worth thousands."

"But it always will be worth that. In fact, the longer you sit on it, the higher the price it will fetch in the end. And Tom was your dad's friend. He told me they used to play together as boys, long before he worked here. Your dad's dream would never have meant doing the dirty on Tom."

Patty sighed suddenly. "So what are you proposing?"

"Give me a chance to make Puzzle work for you. See if he really can turn things around. If we can drum up enough custom for you to make a decent living here, promise me you'll let Tom live out his days in his own place, amongst everything he loves."

There was a long silence. In the hall, a Grandfather clock chimed another hour away. Outside, a blood-red sunset spilled across the sky. Birds swooped, swift and silent, into the safety of the darkening trees.

Dad must have finished packing up ages ago. He'd be wondering what Nicky was up to. And when he found out that his son was busy negotiating away the chance of a really big land clearance job, he wasn't likely to pat him on the back for it. But Nicky pushed the thought aside. If this worked, he didn't have to tell Dad. With a bit of luck, he might never find out.

"OK." Patty spoke quietly, getting up from the table and coming across to stand beside him by the window. "You win – for now, anyway. To be honest, I've never really wanted to develop that land – I've got too many memories attached to it. But if Puzzle doesn't do well, or if the customers still don't come, then I'll have to go back to the development plan idea. I won't have any choice."

Nicky nodded, but his voice was rough as sandpaper when he answered. "Leave it to me. I'll do everything I can to make it work."

14

"How come you're not practising? You've only got just over a week left."

Nicky reined Puzzle in and looked at Lynette, struggling with his temper. "I took him through the woods. I can't be jumping him every second. He'll burn out." Nicky didn't add that he'd been to see Tom, to check he was OK. Tom didn't seem to be getting any better, but at least he wasn't any worse.

"Anyway, Patty wants you in the tack room once you get him stabled. She's sorted out some clothes for you to try on."

"You're joking, aren't you?" Nicky's fists closed tight on the reins.

"You surely didn't think we'd let you ride in the gymkhana in jeans and a sweatshirt. You'll need

79

jodhpurs and a hat as well. You're supposed to be representing a riding school, not a ranch from the wild west."

Nicky backed Puzzle up a few steps. "You do what you have to with Puzzle. You can plait his mane. You can give him a fluffy nose band. You can stick gold stars all over his hooves if you want. He's easy going, and he'll like the attention. But I am *not* dressing up like a gorgio. Not for anybody!"

"Is there a problem?" Patty appeared out of the tack room, a blue jacket and jodhpurs hung over her arm.

"Nicky intends to take Puzzle to the show looking like a cow hand." Lynette turned back to him. "They won't realize you're in the jumping event. They'll probably direct you off to the kids' fancy dress competition."

"Better than looking like a flipping Barbie doll that can't even stay on his back."

"OK, OK. That'll do." Patty stepped between them. "I'm afraid you have to look the part, Nicky. It's BHS regulations. You'd be disqualified otherwise. And you'll need a hat, even when you're not competing, from now on."

"I never wear a hat."

"It's a school rule. In fact, it's the law, for insurance and everything. And if we're trying to set an example to younger children, we must show them the right way to protect themselves. You'd feel awful if anyone ever got a head injury because they were trying to be cool like Nicky Ghiselli."

Nicky shrugged. "OK, then. But I'm only wearing that stuff in shows. It'll be just a hat the rest of the time."

"So, how's the practice going, anyway?" asked Patty brightly. "Are you going to come over every day next week, during half term?"

"All except Tuesday. It's my sister's birthday, and I'll have to be at home for that."

"He can take Puzzle for a practice now," Lynette cut in. "I got the jumps all set up for him earlier, and he's only been out for a ride through the woods. Puzzle must be burning to do something more interesting."

"I'm trying to let him take things a bit easy…"

"Don't be so wimpish. That horse loves to jump. I reckon if you put him in a field of jumps with no rider at all, he'd still go over them happily."

Nicky shot her a black look, but he nudged Puzzle forward, through the gate and across into the field. Lynette was probably right about Puzzle not minding too much, anyway. So far, since he'd started training him last weekend, they hadn't had a single pole down. He coped with doubles, with spreads, and even the triple – although, with his funny lurching style, it meant he had to get over each one from an absolute standstill.

"Come on then, boy," Nicky whispered gently. "Let's show them what we can do."

15

It rained all day on Tuesday.

"How many have you got coming?" asked Mum, looking dubiously out of the trailer window. She'd been planning a barbecue, but they'd all have to stay inside now.

Sabrina took some coloured clay out of the "Jewels and Jewellery" set Mum and Dad had given her, and began shaping a delicate-looking flower brooch as a prize for some party game she'd planned. "Just Kelly and Carla. I did ask some others, but they were all busy."

"I suppose that's not too many muddy footprints," Mum sighed.

"That's not fair. I didn't want to have it here in the first place. I wanted to go to the pub."

Mum sighed. "You know we can't afford to chuck money about at the moment."

Nicky paused from blowing up balloons. "Where do you want these?"

"Just hang them in bunches all around. And can you put a couple outside, on the tow-bar? I've seen other people have them on gates outside their houses."

"What time are they coming?" Nicky, wiping the rain from his face, came back in from tying the balloons outside. He wouldn't tell Sabrina but, with the wind bouncing them against the sides of the trailer, they weren't going to last long anyway.

"About four o'clock. Kelly said that was the time her party started."

Nicky raised his eyebrows. "Well, thank goodness we've got her to help and advise us."

Mum shot him a warning glance, but Sabrina didn't notice. She was pressing sequins into the flower brooch, and fixing a safety pin to the back.

By half-past four Sabrina was looking anxiously out of the window, wondering if she'd got the time wrong.

By half-past five she had walked out in the rain to the edge of the site twice, worrying that she'd told them the wrong day.

At six o'clock she wrenched the safety pin off the

back of the flower brooch, and burst all the balloons with it.

Mum put sausages and bread rolls on to fine china plates, but Dad and Jim, arriving home drenched and dripping from a day's logging, were the only ones who ate them.

Nicky suddenly announced that he was going out to Mill Farm. "There's only two days to the show," he explained. "I need to make sure everything's ready for Thursday."

It wasn't true, of course. Lynette had everything completely organized. All Nicky had to do was turn up. But he just couldn't bear to listen to Sabrina crying any longer.

16

"You both look really smart." Bretta Miles came riding through the maze of trucks, vans and horse boxes to where Nicky was sitting. "I wish I'd plaited Eclipse's mane now."

Nicky pulled a face and looked down at the dark blue jacket and jodhpurs. "I feel like a prat. And all Puzzle's ribbons and stuff are Lynette's idea. She was determined to make us both look like idiots."

He got up and stood close to Bretta's horse, Eclipse, rubbing the black Arab's forehead as she pressed her nose warmly against him.

Puzzle followed, and Nicky stood back as the two horses faced each other, their ears pricked forward, sniffing and snorting. Bretta had come over to Mill Farm last week, to watch Nicky jump Puzzle, but this was the first time their horses had met. Suddenly Puzzle stretched his neck out and nuzzled at Eclipse's rich black mane, curling back his front lip and nibbling her gently. Eclipse arched her neck, and blew softly back.

Bretta grinned, and stroked Eclipse. "Friends," she said firmly.

"Friends," Nicky agreed. He put his arm round Puzzle, and gave him a hug.

"There's still an hour till our event. Shall we go and try them over the practice jump?"

"We'll come and watch you," said Nicky. "But I'm not sure if it's good for Puzzle to do too much practice. He sweated up a bit when I rode him yesterday. Once we've got these half-term shows out the way, I'll tell Lynette that she's pushing too hard."

Nicky turned away, tightening a loose ribbon in Puzzle's mane. It was true – he did think Lynette was wanting too much too soon, but that wasn't the whole reason why he wasn't wild about trying the practice jump. He knew other riders and spectators would be milling about, and the idea of being watched, or maybe Puzzle being laughed at, was making him all knotty inside.

He followed Bretta and Eclipse. Puzzle walked behind, his nose pressing into Nicky's back. They passed the tea tent, and the pet show, and a few stalls

87

selling local crafts. Nicky didn't hold on to Puzzle. He didn't need to.

Just a few times Puzzle stopped. Once to sniff at an elderly lady's yellow straw hat. Once to avoid a terrier that slipped its lead and ran barking and yapping between his legs. And once when a little elf-like girl with huge hazel eyes dropped her ice-cream and burst into tears.

That third time, Nicky stopped too.

The girl's mother, a gentle-faced woman with eyes the soft grey of wood-pigeons, was behind a stall selling carved ornaments and bits of old furniture. She put down the little cart-horse she was chiselling, hugged her daughter and pointed to Puzzle. "That horse is looking at you, Emily. Do you want to say 'hello'?" She held out her daughter's hand towards Puzzle, wiping away the sticky mess that was dripping down the front of the girl's dungarees at the same time.

Puzzle sniffed the outstretched fingers.

Nicky glanced back, and stopped. "It's OK. He's very gentle."

"Can I ride him?" Emily stopped crying and squinted up at her mum.

"Don't be silly, sweetheart…"

Emily's eyes shone bright with tears again.

"I'm sorry," her mum looked apologetically at Nicky. "We've been up since the crack of dawn getting the stall ready. It's a long day for her sometimes."

"No problem." Nicky glanced at the stall, jumbled with carved ornaments and household bits and pieces. "Did you make all this yourself?"

Emily's mum nodded. "I do up old furniture too."

Nicky tilted his head to look at her. "You're not Annie Hobbs, are you? The carpenter woman?"

She smiled. "That's right. How did you know about me?"

"My dad. Joseph Ghiselli. He's done a bit of work for you lately."

Annie's smile glowed brighter, and she held out her hand. "Of course. You must be Nicky. He's talked a lot about you."

"Mum – please let me ride him. *Please!*"

Annie hesitated and looked at Nicky. "She's horse mad…"

"She'll be quite safe." Nicky knelt down swiftly, lifting Emily up on to Puzzle's back. She gave a bubbling laugh, her hands gripping tightly to the mane as, swishing his tail lazily, Puzzle followed on behind Bretta and Eclipse. Emily was still chattering and laughing when Annie finally lifted her off and led her back to the stall.

Nicky leaned on the rope that cordoned off the practice area, watching Bretta join the other riders who were circling round. Some of them looked knotted with nerves, others were cool and confident.

Suddenly, Nicky's eye was caught by an iron-grey hunter, stomping and prancing over near the trees. Its rider, a lanky, lizard faced man in a black jacket, was laying into it with his crop, reining it back at the same time. The horse tossed its head, its whole body sticky with sweat. Nicky felt the swish and sting of the crop each time it cut into the horse's side. "Hey!" he ducked under the rope and ran over, but as soon as he got near the man flicked his hooded eyes coldly in Nicky's direction, and rode away.

Unsettled, Nicky went back to Puzzle, leaning against him and letting the horse's calm, solid manner settle the anger that was twisting through him. "Some people ought to be banned from keeping a horse," he muttered. Puzzle pushed at him with his nose and rubbed his whiskery chin across his shoulders. Nicky softened, the anger melting. He couldn't save every horse in the world, but at least Puzzle was safe from monsters like that.

A pale-faced girl appeared on a snow-white pony. She cantered him at the jump, jabbed at his mouth, then ended up halfway along his neck as he came to a sudden stop at the pole. She lost her stirrups and fumbled about while her pony ambled away to the side and began tearing at a clump of bushes. "Oh, stop it!" She yanked at the reins, forcing his head up, and pulled him round to face the jump again. By the third refusal, the girl was sniffing loudly as she trotted near to where Nicky was watching.

"This is my first competition. Is it yours too?" Nicky nodded across at her and smiled.

"Does it show?" The girl wiped her white-gloved hand across her cheek and looked at him. She squinted down at Nicky. "Don't I know you?"

"You'll probably remember my horse more easily."

The girl glanced at Puzzle, and her expression cleared. "I've got it. You're from that riding school. We went there to look at this horse. He wasn't quite…"

"You said he looked like he'd been crossed with a cow," Nicky said softly.

A pink flush flooded the pale skin. "I'm sorry. My mum was winding me up. You know what it's like."

"Doesn't matter now. I had a chat with him about it later, and I told him it was your loss, not his." Nicky grinned suddenly as she stared at him, not sure whether he was joking or not. "Your name's Jade, isn't it?"

"That's right. You've got a good memory. I can't remember yours."

"Nicky. And this is Puzzle." He put out his hand for her pony to sniff his fingers. "I see you got what you wanted anyway. A grey one."

Jade pulled a face. "He's called Ice-Cream Cherry Sundae – I call him 'Cherry' for short. When we bought him, the owner said he was a good jumper, but he's hopeless. He won't do anything I tell him." She pulled him round again, jerking her hands so hard that Cherry's mouth was wrenched wide open.

Nicky winced, but he spoke gently. "Will you give me five minutes with him? I might be able to sort him out."

Jade looked doubtful. "I can't see what good five minutes would do. He must have had a lifetime of playing up." She hesitated, then slid off, handing the reins to Nicky. "I suppose you may as well try. I'm supposed to be jumping in about ten minutes."

Nicky dropped Puzzle's reins, and stood sideways on to Cherry, staring ahead. "The first trick is not to look at him straight away. Not to threaten him. That way he comes to you when he's ready – you haven't had to force him into anything."

After a moment, Nicky stepped forward. Cherry followed. Nicky stopped. Cherry stopped. Nicky stepped forward. Cherry followed. Nicky stopped. Cherry stopped. "See how he's trusting me? He wants to be with me. He's making a choice for himself."

Next Nicky walked all round Cherry, running his hands over his legs, picking up his hooves, and stroking his shoulders and quarters. Despite his pretty looks and colouring, his underneath was splattered with dried mud, and his mane and tail were knotted up. "Do you groom him much?"

"I don't get time. I started at private school this term, and there's masses of homework…"

"In the wild, horses are always grooming each other. It's part of belonging to a herd. And it's a way of caring. A way of trusting."

"…I've got ballet lessons on Tuesdays, and swimming Wednesdays and Fridays. I've been picked for the squad, so there's loads of extra training to do. Then, on Saturdays I do violin…"

"If you groom him, he'll get to know you better. You'll be his friend. You'll be part of his herd."

"It's just that…"

"Everywhere he's letting me touch him now are his vulnerable spots. In the wild, being touched in some of those places might mean he's being attacked. Lions go for the neck. Wild dogs go for the back legs and belly. Sometimes they tear open a horse's stomach and follow the trail of the intestines…"

"Stop it. You're making me feel sick." Jade

looked whiter than ever, but at least Nicky knew she was listening at last.

"And see this spot here, just between his eyes?" Nicky reached up and rubbed his forefinger in a slow, circular motion, anti-clockwise.

"What about it?"

"If he's letting me in here, he feels really safe. Because his eyes are set at the side, he can't actually get a good view of what I'm doing, so he's got to be very careful about who he lets touch him there."

Jade still looked doubtful. "My friend Vicki says you have to blow up horses' nostrils to bond with them properly, but I couldn't bear that. It sounds disgusting."

Nicky laughed. "Horses have a powerful sense of smell. Blowing up their noses helps them to get a good whiff of you, but I'm not sure they really like it. I mean – would you?"

Jade pulled a face. "I don't suppose I'd be begging for more." She hesitated. "Look, will you try him for me, then? Just over the practice jump. See if it's worked."

"Hang on to Puzzle then. He'll probably want to follow me." Nicky passed her Puzzle's reins, then sprang on to Cherry's back. The stirrups were too short to bother with, so he crossed them over the pony's neck. "First – you've got to try and relax. A horse knows when you're uptight, and if he thinks you're worried, he'll be worried too. And keep a light hand on the reins. In fact, when you get a bit more confident, you may find you don't need them at all." And to prove his point, Nicky knotted them and pushed them away up Cherry's neck. Then, just guiding him with the soft touch of his legs, and talking gently, Nicky cantered towards the jump. They cleared it three times. As Nicky turned him back to Jade, Cherry trotted freely. His neck was arched and his ears were flicking. "Watch his ears," Nicky called. "When they're like that, it means he's tuned in to his rider."

"He looks ... really different." Jade took the reins back off Nicky shyly. "I've never seen him look that lovely before."

"Well, good luck." Nicky smiled at her. "I'll come over and see how you get on."

He watched as she jogged away towards the ring, still struggling to keep her feet in the stirrups. But he noticed with relief that she wasn't jabbing at Cherry's mouth any more.

He walked with Puzzle over to the ringside, and waited for Jade's number to be called. Puzzle stood quietly beside him, occasionally blowing softly or nibbling the collar at the back of his jacket.

"Look – it's Cherry now." Nicky pointed them out to Puzzle as Cherry and Jade entered the ring. They got twenty-four faults, and Jade fell off at the end when Cherry shied suddenly at a stray paper bag. She got back up, brushing the mud and grass off her crisp cream jodhpurs, and indicated to the judges that she was retiring. But as she picked up the reins, ready to lead Cherry out, Nicky saw her stop suddenly, turn, and rub him gently between the eyes.

He grinned to himself. Perhaps the last ten minutes had done some good. And at least in that time he hadn't been worrying about what was coming next.

"Nicky – this event's nearly finished. They'll be calling you to walk the course in a minute. Shall I hold Puzzle for you?"

"No thanks. I'm keeping him with me. I need a friendly face around."

"But ... nobody ever takes their *horse* with them. It's meant to be just the riders..." Patty's voice trailed away as she watched Nicky and Puzzle walk away from her, and into the arena with the other competitors. Puzzle went where Nicky went. And when Nicky stopped, Puzzle stopped. And at every jump, as Nicky bent to examine it, Puzzle snorted and blew on it carefully.

All around her, Patty could see people taking interest. Some were pointing. A few were laughing. One competitor, a stooped, lanky man in a black hunting jacket, went over to the judge's caravan, waving his arms and beating the air with his fist. Patty couldn't hear what he was saying, but she knew who he was – Melvyn Leach, a rich horse trainer with a poor reputation. From where Patty was standing, Melvyn didn't look impressed. He flicked his crop angrily against the rope, and then swung round and pointed it at Puzzle. Patty guessed he was arguing that a horse walking the course should be against the rules. Except that, where Melvyn Leach was concerned, rules weren't usually high on his list of things to worry about.

She chewed on her fingernails, hunched her shoulders up, and raised her eyebrows. "Oh well, Nicky Ghiselli," she said under her breath, "I suppose you're the expert for the day. But if you're going to be this different, if you're going to draw this much attention to us, then you'd better be good. You'd better be really, really good…"

17

"*A*nd next, Number 223, Nicky Ghiselli from Mill Farm Riding School, riding Puzzle…*"*

As they entered the ring, Nicky felt sick. He couldn't even remember where the first jump was, let alone the order of the course. The buzzer went and he circled twice. He wouldn't be able to do it. He couldn't perform in front of all these people.

Puzzle cantered, his ears flicking, waiting for the command that didn't come. The crowd shifted uncomfortably, sensing that something was wrong. Everything was quiet. From the corner of his eye, Nicky saw Patty watching. She seemed frozen, her hands twisted tight together in a kind of prayer.

The buzzer rang again. If he didn't start soon, he would be eliminated.

Suddenly, cantering round for a third time, Nicky saw Patty turn to talk to someone. He recognized the faded brown jacket and the old corduroy hat. Tom had come! He knew Nicky was competing – Nicky had told him that much, although he'd kept quiet about the reason why. But Tom had seemed pretty washed out two days before. Nicky never dreamed he'd turn up to watch.

"OK, boy," Nicky leaned forward, whispering in Puzzle's ear. "I've just remembered what we're here for. So let's get on with it!"

Nicky wasn't sure if it was him guiding Puzzle, or Puzzle guiding him, but suddenly they were facing the first jump.

It went in a blur, Puzzle bounding eagerly round the course, flicking his funny stub of a tail as he lurched over the gate, the double, the triple and the wall. Nicky leant forward, concentrating on each jump. They could have been leaping fallen palm trees on a desert island. Nicky forgot about the crowds. He forgot about Patty. He even forgot about Tom. It was just him and Puzzle, and a job to do.

"And that was a clear round for Nicky Ghiselli..."

"Brilliant!" Bretta, waiting for her number to be called, waved as he trotted out of the ring. "There's been a couple of other clear rounds, but at least you'll be in the jump-off."

"That was smashing." Patty appeared, followed

by Tom. Other people were gathering too, patting Puzzle's neck. Some of the faces Nicky knew. It was a local show, and half his school seemed to have come just for something to do.

"I like your horse, Nicky. He's a real joker."

"I don't know how you stayed on. Did you put superglue on his saddle or something?"

Nicky nodded at them, then slid off and leant against Puzzle. He wasn't quite sure what to say. He didn't usually talk much to the others at school. And more than that, they didn't usually talk much to him.

But watching Bretta take Eclipse on the fourth clear round of the event, he felt a sudden ripple of excitement spread through him. It wasn't about winning. He wanted to win, but that was for Tom and Patty's sake, not for his. But just being in that ring, having to focus, knowing he had done well at the end, filled him with a buzz he hadn't expected to feel.

When the competitors for the jump-off were called, he was almost looking forward to it.

The jumps were higher this time, but they weren't a problem. Puzzle leapt round them happily, and Nicky was settled enough for it to feel like fun.

Moving round the course, he was aware of the crowd pressed tight against the rope. People called out, wishing him luck, urging him on.

And if Nicky was starting to relax, Puzzle was glowing. When spectators called his name, he tossed his head. When they clapped, he gave a funny, prancing little dance. At every jump, there was a gasp, and then a roar of approval.

"You great show-off," Nicky grinned as he leaned along Puzzle's neck, turning him towards the final jump. It was a wall, built to look like a castle, and higher than anything they had tackled so far back at Mill Farm.

It was then that it happened – a squeal and a shriek from close by.

"Nicky! Nicky! Nicky!"

His eyes caught on two girls standing only metres away, jiggling and waving madly. "Nicky! Nicky! Nicky!"

It was Carla and Kelly.

The memory of last Tuesday flashed through his mind – ending with Sabrina curled up with a cushion, crying through the whole evening. He'd gone out to look for the two girls on his way back from Mill Farm, but they weren't hanging around in any of their usual haunts, and Sabrina begged him to leave it when he told her he'd sort them out in school next week.

Now he raised his fist in their direction, just as Puzzle began to rise up. Too late, Nicky turned his attention back to the jump. Puzzle, feeling the movement and sensing the sudden change in mood, faltered slightly. His front hoof tipped the brick in the centre of the wall. A disappointed groan rumbled through the crowd as it toppled to the ground.

"...*And that was four faults for Nicky Ghiselli on Puzzle, which sadly puts them out of the competition...*"

Nicky rode slowly back towards Patty and Tom. His eyes scanned the muddle of faces, looking for Kelly and Carla. He wouldn't blame them for cutting into his concentration. That was his own fault for letting himself waver. But in spite of what Sabrina wanted, when he caught up with them he'd let them know what he thought of pumped-up little girls who broke his sister's heart for fun.

"You did well. That last wall was really high, and Puzzle very nearly made it..." Patty hurried over and walked along beside him.

"It wasn't Puzzle's fault we took that brick off. I unbalanced him at the last minute. It upset his rhythm."

"The crowd loved him. It was like they were watching a show, not a jump-off. Several people came over to comment while he was going round. I know he's got an odd way about him, but he does get noticed."

Tom appeared, and Puzzle nosed a packet of

peppermints out of his pocket. Tom laughed. "I brought them specially," he winked, "because you're a bit of a star."

Nicky, relieved that Patty didn't seem to think it was the end of the world that they hadn't won, turned back to watch the lizard–faced man ride in to stand in first place.

"That's Melvyn Leach," Tom murmured. "Watch him smile when the judge goes up to him. People say he's got teeth like a crocodile."

Bretta joined him on Eclipse, to collect the second prize.

Melvyn's horse, Bullet, moved restlessly, shying away as the judge passed up the rosette. Nicky winced. Even from across the field, he could tell that the hunter was more used to blows than soft words.

He was suddenly glad it was all over for today. He couldn't even be bothered to think about Kelly and Carla any more. He ran his hands down Puzzle's shoulders and on to his legs. He was hot and sweaty, and looked like he'd had enough too. "Come on, mate. Let's get you rubbed down and back in the box. I'll catch up with those two vixens another day."

18

"Y ou'll have to do better than that next time. You've got another show on Sunday, and another one next weekend." Lynette drummed her long, varnished fingernails on the stable door as she watched Nicky clean out Puzzle's hooves before he settled him down for the night.

"Patty seemed happy enough. She said we did well for a first time."

"She must be getting soft. The only way this is going to work is if you start winning. Nobody notices a loser."

"You're wrong. Puzzle built up a bit of a fan club this afternoon."

Lynette's eyes narrowed. "I don't want people

noticing you for the wrong reasons either. I'm not running a training school for clowns."

Nicky ran his fingers slowly along the edge of the hoof pick, and watched her turn away. Her thin back was stiff and straight as she marched off up the yard. Suddenly he drew his hand back and hurled the hoof pick after her. It fell short, landing with a clatter on the cobbles. Lynette didn't look round.

He felt Puzzle nuzzle against his shoulder. "I know, I know. That was stupid…" Nicky sighed, collected the hoof pick, and walked back to the stable. "But it wasn't as stupid as it might have been. I'm a pretty good shot. I could have hit her if I'd wanted to."

19

The next show was further away. Nicky was relieved. At least there was less chance of anyone from school hanging around this time.

He had time to kill, so he tied Puzzle in the shade and wandered away on his own. Patty was off somewhere in search of coffee and Lynette had been "too busy" to go with them again.

As he browsed between the saddlers and the popcorn seller, he saw a stall he recognized.

"Hello." Emily, her face half-hidden behind a giant candy floss, was perched on a carved wooden rocking horse.

"Hello!" Nicky walked over, impressed that she remembered him.

"Are you competing again?" Annie Hobbs was sanding down a rickety-looking wheel-back chair.

"In about an hour's time."

"We'll come and watch you if I can find someone to mind the stall. You were great last time."

Nicky shrugged. "I made a mess of things at the end."

"But you were wonderful to watch. You were so … different."

"I cried when you didn't win. Do you want some candyfloss?" Emily thrust the sticky mass at Nicky.

"Better not. I might end up with pink bits in my hair." Nicky grinned at her, then turned back to Annie. "Do you come to all the shows then?"

"As many as I can. I'm trying to build up a name for myself, and this is a good way to get my work seen."

Nicky looked at her stall properly for the first time. She had a few bits of furniture in various stages of repair, but it was the carvings on the table that really drew Nicky. They were mainly animals – beautiful horses, all sorts of birds, a tray of brightly polished insects. At the front she'd put more ordinary things, like wooden napkin rings and pine toilet-roll holders decorated with flowers. "They're great," Nicky nodded. "Especially the animals."

Annie sighed and pushed her walnut brown fringe back out of her eyes. "I love making them, but they don't sell well. They're too expensive really. The other stuff – the things at the front – go better. Are you good with wood?"

Nicky shrugged. "Better than with most things, especially at school. But I s'pose I should be really. I've been working with it all my life."

"Have your family always been woodsmen then?"

"As far back as I know. Trees and horses. That's what runs in our blood."

"I like your horse. He's got kind eyes," Emily cut in again. Then, chewing the last bits of pink floss from off the stick, she added solemnly, "I like your eyes too. They're twinkly when you smile. People are always nice if they've got twinkly eyes."

"Oh Emily!" Annie bent down and began rubbing crystals of sugary pink off her daughter's face with a tissue. She smiled apologetically up at Nicky. "I'm afraid she says what she thinks."

"Well, I'm glad she does. That's the best thing anyone's said to me for ages." Nicky laughed suddenly. "But I'd better get going. Puzzle might be worried that I've got lost."

He gave a brief wave and walked away, leaving Emily rocking wildly, while Annie rummaged for a cloth to start waxing the chair.

* * *

Puzzle was on top form again. If anything, he jumped even higher than before, as if the memory of the knocked brick was a mistake he was determined not to repeat.

They were about to go out after another clear round when Puzzle swung suddenly to the left, cantered to the other end of the ring, and stopped. On the grass lay a yellow straw hat. Behind the rope, a few metres away, an elderly lady was leaning forward, trying to reach it. "Oh no you don't." Nicky battled to pull Puzzle's head up, muttering, "You've got muscles like iron. And a will to match."

Puzzle ignored him, stretching his neck and lifting the hat almost lovingly between his teeth. He raised his head, looking round like a magician showing off a dove he'd just pulled from his sleeve. Then, prancing slightly, he trotted over towards the lady.

"I'm so sorry…" Nicky stammered, as Puzzle stood in front of her, the hat dangling from his mouth. "I hope he hasn't made it too soggy."

Very gravely, the lady took the hat from Puzzle, turned it over carefully to examine it, then fixed it firmly back on her head. "Not at all," she said, a sparkle suddenly lighting her faded blue eyes. Then she nodded at Puzzle. "I really am most grateful to you."

Only then, with a toss of his head, did Puzzle let

Nicky guide him back out of the ring, flicking his tail proudly as the new applause rang in their ears.

Once they were through the exit, people pressed round them.

"Is he yours?"

"How on earth do you stay on?"

"He bounces higher than a kangaroo!"

Puzzle was hugged and patted. Children ran and pulled him handfuls of long grass from the edge of the field. Emily made him a daisy chain. And he posed for photographs, wrinkling back his top lip and thrusting his whiskery nose towards the cameras as if he was laughing.

"You'll have to learn to write your own name," whispered Nicky, as everyone drifted away at last. "I reckon they'll start asking you for autographs soon."

The commentator's announcement caught everyone's attention,

"And now, in a jump-off against the clock, we have three competitors. And first to jump will be Nicky Ghiselli on Puzzle…"

A small cheer went up, and as Nicky rode off towards the enclosure, people hurried to get a place with a good view.

They did their best, but speed wasn't Puzzle's strong point. They finished third, behind Melvyn

Leach's Bullet – who, wild-eyed and snorting, tore round the course as if he was being chased by devils – and an immaculately turned-out black stallion that looked like it modelled for bank adverts in its spare time.

"Third's good," Patty smiled encouragingly. "Third gets our name in the paper. Go in and get your prize."

Nicky stood beside Puzzle while the judge walked between them, handing out the first and second rosettes. Puzzle was blowing a bit, and Nicky wanted to give him a break from being ridden.

As the judge turned to them, his mouth turned down like someone sucking on a slice of lemon. "An unusual-looking animal. And an unusual ... er ... technique."

Nicky's back stiffened. He knew the tone. He knew the meaning. His expression became wooden, and he didn't answer. From the corner of his eye he saw the judge reluctantly offer the rosette to him. Nicky would have loved to tell him to keep it. Or, better still, where to stick it. But Lynette would want it for her office wall, and he had to keep playing the game. And in that moment, as Nicky hesitated, Puzzle stretched out his neck towards the judge, gently took the rosette from him with his teeth, and pressed it against Nicky's chest.

It hung like a green medal on his blue jacket, and Nicky grabbed it just in time before it slipped to the ground.

"Well, I…" The judge began to stutter, but his words were drowned by the cheer that rose like a wave from the watching crowd.

If they'd liked Puzzle before, they loved him now.

And it was a close-up picture of Puzzle, the green rosette held between his teeth, that made front-page news in the evening paper that night.

20

"Y ou'll have to go faster than that next time." Lynette stood and watched as Nicky hosed Puzzle down next morning.

Nicky glanced at her, wondering what she was doing here. School was closed for an extra day, so he'd been able to come over, but Lynette usually took her day off on a Monday. He'd been looking forward to having her out of the way.

She was done up funny too. She was wearing tight cream jodhpurs and a black show jacket. Her hair was twisted high into a bun, and her thin lips were shaped with strawberry-red lipstick. He wondered if she was planning to muck out the stables like that, but he swallowed back the question. "He's not built for speed. Surely even you can see that."

"There's still things you can do. You can cut corners. You can take a more diagonal route between jumps."

"It's dangerous. He needs a chance to judge distance and height."

The strawberry-red lips tightened. "You'll have to give it a try. I'm expecting you to win next time."

Nicky was about to answer, when a car rolled into the yard. A woman with cropped, bleached hair, and a man with a ponytail, got out.

"Hi. I'm Suzi Finn, and this is Kris, the photographer. I rang yesterday about doing a short interview…"

"Fine. No problem." Lynette graced them with a smile like sugar candy, and touched her hair.

"Is this the horse?" Suzi glanced at Puzzle and pulled out her notebook.

"That's him. As you can see, the stable boy's still getting him ready, but if you want to come with me, I'll show you round Mill Farm while we're waiting."

Nicky worked at Puzzle furiously, half tempted to rub mud into, rather than out of, his coat. Puzzle, sensing Nicky's mood, picked up one of the brushes that were lying about in the yard and began waving it in the air. It usually made Nicky laugh, but today he didn't even notice.

"Hey, that's great." Kris was back. He walked all

round Puzzle, clicking the camera from different angles.

"Perhaps you could go and muck out the other stables." Lynette appeared suddenly with Suzi, still smiling sweetly. "I'll finish Puzzle off for you."

"Catch." Nicky threw the curry-comb at her so hard she had to duck. He didn't look at any of them as he strode off to get the spade and the wheelbarrow.

21

At school the next day Nicky had the local newspapers thrust in his face as soon as he walked through the gate. "That's your horse, isn't it?" "You were great last week in that competition!" "Can you teach me to ride?"

Sabrina came over waving two newspapers at break time. "Kelly and Carla asked if you'd sign your name on these."

Bretta, who was sitting on the step with Nicky, leaned across and read the headlines out loud:

PUZZLE CLEANS UP AFTER THE SHOW

STARS OF THE STABLES

One of the papers showed Puzzle waving the grooming brush about between his teeth, while the other one had Lynette, the strawberry-red mouth stretched into a dazzling smile, standing beside Puzzle with the green rosette pinned to her jacket.

Nicky pushed the papers away angrily. "Tell Kelly and Carla to come over here themselves. I want a word with them anyway."

"Leave it, Nicky. It was a mistake last Tuesday. They've been fine today. Don't stir it up again."

Nicky looked at Sabrina, his expression softening, and sighed. "OK. But I'm not signing their papers for them. Just tell them I haven't got a pen."

"Are you all right?" Bretta looked at Nicky anxiously as Sabrina pulled a face at him and left.

Nicky laced his fingers together, pushing against the bones till they clicked. "I just don't like all this newspaper stuff."

"But it's what Lynette wants, isn't it? Lots of publicity?"

"I know." Nicky was quiet, staring across at a flock of seagulls that swooped suddenly down on to the school field towards an empty crisp packet. "I just wish I didn't have to be part of it."

Someone tapped his shoulder. Turning round, he saw Carla standing gazing at him like a puppy that wants its tummy rubbed. "I found a pen," she said.

Nicky rolled his eyes at Bretta, sighed, then took the papers off her. "Just don't mess my sister about again," he said, as he scrawled his name across the corner of the photographs. He handed the papers back without looking up.

Lynette actually sounded friendly when Nicky cycled over that evening. "It's going really well," she said, in such a honeyed voice that Nicky wondered where the poison was hidden.

It didn't take him long to find out.

As he got Puzzle out to take him over the jumps in the field, Lynette followed them. She had something in her hand.

"What's that?"

"A stop watch."

"I don't want it. I told you, Puzzle does his best. I'm not going to start timing him."

"You don't have a choice." Lynette settled herself down on a pile of old tyres in the middle of the field. The soft honey voice was already gone. "This 'joke horse' stuff is OK for a while, but it's going to wear thin if you're always second best. You have to start winning if you're going to keep the interest going."

Nicky tried to ignore her, cantering round the field, taking Puzzle towards each jump in his own time.

"Faster! Faster! That was twenty-two seconds. You could cut at least five off if you make more effort."

Nicky ignored her again, and this time, when he finished, she was almost screaming. "It won't do. It was just the same as last time. You've got to keep pushing!"

Temper suddenly flared up in him. "You ride him then!" he shouted back. "You risk breaking his leg, or twisting his spine. I'm damn sure I'm not going to be the one to hurt him!" Leaping off, he flung the reins at her and stormed away.

All that night, Nicky couldn't sleep. He'd made a real mess of things, shouting at Lynette. The only good thing was that she wouldn't have been able to keep going once he'd gone – she couldn't ride Puzzle herself, so at least she couldn't really have got her talons into him.

It was a shame, really. If she could manage to ride him, she'd have more chance of finding out that she was wrong. Puzzle was already doing his best. He really couldn't go any faster.

But that weekend, at a show thirty kilometres away, in a timed jump-off between Nicky riding Puzzle and Melvyn Leach on Bullet, Puzzle came away with the first prize.

22

"Kelly wants to know if Bretta Miles is your girlfriend."

"We're just mates." Nicky leaned over Sabrina's shoulder to watch her colour in an ugly grey bird, its long scraggy neck tangled in a broken fishing net. "Not that it's any of her business."

Sabrina glanced up at him. "She asks lots of questions about you. They both do."

"What sort of questions?"

"What your favourite pop group is. If you like chocolate. Whether you're a good swimmer or not."

"Well, just don't tell them what colour my underpants are." Nicky crashed on to the seat and closed his eyes. He'd been up to Mill Farm before school that morning, and now he had a load of

120

spellings to learn before he went to help Jim outside.

"They've already asked me." Sabrina cut into his thoughts.

"Who's asked you what?"

"Kelly and Carla. About your underpants."

Nicky opened his eyes again. "So what did you tell them?"

Sabrina grinned. "I only mentioned the purple ones with the green hippos. Oh, and those yellow ones with zigzags..." She ducked suddenly as a cushion came flying across the trailer. "Watch it. You'll spoil my new poster."

"What you doing hanging round with them again anyway?" Nicky grew serious. "They haven't done you a lot of favours in the past."

"They're good friends, honestly. Look..." Sabrina picked up her pencil case and rummaged for a moment. "Carla gave me this today. She didn't want anything for it, but I'll try and give her something back."

Nicky leaned forward and took a pot of glittery pink eye shadow off her. The lid was cracked, and the make up inside had gone crusty along the top. "It's not exactly new, is it?"

"So what? It's the thought that counts." Sabrina snatched it back off him and shoved it sulkily back into the pencil case.

Nicky watched her for a moment, taking in her clear olive skin and dark, almond-shaped eyes. "You don't need that muck anyway. You're fine as you are."

"Kelly and Carla wear it."

"Only because they'd look like the two ugly sisters without it."

"You're really mean. I don't say horrible things about Bretta, do I?"

Nicky hesitated. "No. OK. I'm sorry."

"They've asked me to go into town on the bus tomorrow. After school. They go every Friday because it's late-night shopping."

Outside, Nicky heard someone draw up. From the burble of the engine, he knew it wasn't Mum or Dad coming back from getting the shopping. He glanced out of the window to see a man getting out of a green Land Rover. He walked over to Jim, who was sorting out long, supple hazel sticks that Annie had suggested he might weave to make baskets or bins. They chatted for a while, and then Jim pointed towards the trailer.

A moment later there was a knock at the door.

Reluctantly, Nicky went outside to see what the visitor wanted.

"Hi! I'm Harjit Gopal, *Horse and Rider* magazine. I expect you've heard of us."

"I don't read stuff like that."

"No? OK – well, we're a monthly mag for 'horsey' souls. We cover everything – problem horses, veterinary advice, what tack to buy – all that sort of thing…" He leaned back inside his Land Rover and pulled out a small stack of magazines. "Here. You can keep these. You might find some of the articles quite interesting."

"Thanks." Nicky took the pile from him and put them behind the door of the trailer. Sabrina might like to cut out the pictures, and he certainly wasn't going to let on to Harjit Gopal that trying to read anything, for him, was harder than trying to crack a secret Egyptian code. He wished it was different, but he'd missed so much school when they were travelling around, and reading and writing never seemed very important in those days. "What do you want?"

Harjit Gopal offered him his hand suddenly. "I'd like to talk to you."

"What about?"

"I've just come from Mill Farm Riding School. We'd been getting reports about this 'wonder horse' and I wanted to do a piece on him. I've got some great pictures of the horse jumping – he was amazing to watch – but the manager there said we might get an interesting angle on you too. She said you were a Gypsy."

"Oh, did she?" Nicky's eyes narrowed. He was

proud of what he was, but trust Lynette to use it just to get a better story.

"I'm sorry ... maybe I should have rung first..."

Nicky felt awkward. He didn't seem a bad bloke. He looked young and cheerful, with twinkly brown eyes. As he hesitated a memory clicked in his head – Emily Hobbs on the rocking horse, waving her candy floss at him. He grinned suddenly, remembering what she'd said that day. It was all right to like people with twinkly eyes. "OK then." He stood back to let Harjit Gopal into the trailer. "Ask me whatever you like. I can always refuse to answer. But no photographs."

Harjit Gopal shook his hand again. "Whatever you say," he grinned, and stepped inside.

23

It wasn't until much later that the thoughts began to trickle into Nicky's head.

He lay in bed, listening to Jim snoring, and going back over all the things Harjit Gopal had asked him.

Outside, rain was beginning to rattle down on the roof of the trailer. He pulled himself up on one elbow, looking out at the night through a gap in the curtains. It was sheeting down, smacking against the window like someone aiming a hose pipe.

Nicky sighed and lay his head back on the pillow again. He never much minded the rain, but it would make the going harder for Puzzle if the ground was all slippy. He tried to push the thought away – there never seemed much point battling against things he couldn't control – and ran through the interview with Harjit Gopal again.

Suddenly, a new thought washed over him, making him sit up and stare ahead in the darkness. Early on, when Harjit Gopal had first arrived, he said something that Nicky let pass at the time.

"...*I've got some great pictures of the horse jumping...*"

So how had he got those? Had Lynette ridden him? It wasn't like her to risk coming unseated in front of a camera. After all, twinkly eyes or not, the bloke was a gorgio reporter. He would use whatever picture was the most interesting.

Nicky played out the conversation again, trying to get it to make more sense.

He supposed Harjit Gopal might have got it off one of those other papers, but that wasn't what he'd said. He said he'd *taken* some pictures, and that Puzzle was amazing to watch.

The rain outside turned to hailstones, battering the trailer so that even Jim stirred in his sleep.

Nicky didn't notice any of it.

Thoughts were rushing through his head like a dam bursting. Lynette must have someone else over there – someone at Mill Farm that she was training to cope with Puzzle. And once they were good enough, once she was sure it was safe to let them loose in public, it would be 'goodbye Nicky' all over again.

126

But what could he do about it? The whole thing was swirling past on its own now, and if Lynette had a new rider, nothing he said would matter. She could just carry on without him.

24

If Bretta was surprised to see Nicky turning up on her doorstep before school, she didn't show it.

"When Miss Bullock does the register, can you tell her I threw up on the way in this morning, and had to go back home?"

Bretta hesitated. "I'm not very good at lying…"

"I know. I don't like having to ask you, but it's important."

"OK. But I'm not saying anything else. I'm not going into detail."

"Thanks. You're a real mate. I'll owe you one." Suddenly, as Nicky turned to go, his trainer caught the edge of a piece of garden netting on the side of the path. He stopped for a moment. Suddenly, with a deliberate twist of his foot, he pushed the toe of his trainer into it, threw his arms wide, then faked an elaborate fall on to the wet grass. "Dangerous piece of equipment, that." He sat up, twisting his face into an expression of pure agony, and groaning loudly. "Someone could catch their foot and have a terrible accident."

Bretta stared at him. "What are you on about now?"

Nicky staggered to his feet and groaned again. "You don't have to lie any more. Just change the throwing-up bit. Tell Bullock I was attacked by a wild piece of netting that sprang out at me as I walked innocently past. Tell her you think I've done something horrendous to my leg."

As Nicky turned away, he began limping painfully.

Bretta raised her eyebrows, then laughed and shook her head. "Just don't ever go on the stage." She was still laughing as Nicky grinned back at her, then set off at a run through the gate, and on down the road towards the woods.

25

Nicky had stopped grinning by the time he got to Mill Farm.

He walked quickly down the bridle path that led into the yard, then turned left along a tiny track that ran behind the backs of the stables.

Halfway down he slipped into a gap between the buildings to wait.

There was nobody about. There weren't many rides on a Friday morning, and Lynette was usually up at the house with Patty this time of day.

He could hear the horses chewing, and moving around their stables.

Further along, one horse kept up a continual banging with its hoof against the door. The constant drumming was beginning to get to Nicky.

It reminded him of a dog Grandad had taken in once, a retired greyhound that chewed constantly at its rope, scratching at the ground and whining. Then, as soon as Grandad let it go, it would cower under the trailer, shaking and barking.

Grandad said it was completely stressed – the owners had raced it for too long, run it into the ground. It went completely loopy in the end, howling and snarling at everyone, refusing to let even Grandad get near. When he finally did get hold of it, Grandad ended up with a torn sleeve and a bloody hand. Nicky could still remember the muffled shot that came from over in the woods five minutes later.

It was very wet between the stables. Nicky wished he had on more than his short-sleeved summer shirt. Nettles stung his arms whenever he moved, and the damp seeped in through a split in his trainer. He leant against a stack of rotted logs that were mottled with fungus, trying to get comfortable.

There was a whirr of wheels, then a rattle as a bicycle was leant against the gate opposite. He heard hurried footsteps. Nicky leaned forward, his throat suddenly dry, then breathed out with relief. It was only the postwoman, delivering letters to Lynette's office.

On the wall opposite a small brown spider worked tirelessly on its web, weaving and spinning a lacework of fine silver. Last night's rain dripped steadily from the stable roof, then hung like beads across the sparkling silk. Nicky watched, fascinated. It wasn't a bag of laughs in here, but it was a thousand times better than the maths lesson he was missing.

Suddenly something brushed against his leg. "What the—!" He jumped, then laughed softly. Muffet, the stable cat, sprang on to the log pile and watched him with unblinking yellow eyes. Nicky scratched her ears, glad of the company. There was a chance he could huddle here all day and nothing would happen. Nothing except the endless banging of that hoof against the stable door.

Nicky heard the screech and skid of car tyres up by the house. A car door slammed. There were more footsteps.

Someone else was coming down the yard.

He pressed back against the wall, suddenly aware of the sound of his own breathing.

Muffet, upset that he'd stopped stroking her, complained loudly. Nicky winced, but he didn't move.

The footsteps grew nearer. A shadow fell across the edge of the gap, and someone lanky, slightly stooped, sloped by. He was carrying a bundle – a sort of sack. Nicky felt a creeping unease. It was Melvyn Leach.

"Did you get them?" Nicky couldn't see her, but Lynette's voice – the sugar-sweet one she'd used for the reporters – was unmistakable. She must have been in her office all the time.

"My groom did it. He deals with all of that side of things. Helps me keep the blood off my hands. Verrrry useful." Melvyn laughed. It was an odd, hissing sound.

"Hang on, I'll just put this lot down and I'll take them off you."

"What have you got there anyway? Love letters from your endless admirers?"

Leaning his head back against the damp wall, Nicky rolled his eyes. Melvyn definitely was as slimy as he looked.

Lynette laughed. A high, tinkling laugh. "It's fan mail for Puzzle. He's had loads now."

"Verrrry promising." As Melvyn spoke, Nicky suddenly got a vision of his heavy hooded eyes hardening with interest. "Shall we take them to his lordship?"

"I can't risk it." Lynette laughed again, her voice shriller than ever. "He ate the ones I hung in his stable yesterday. Chewed the corners off. I'm going to hang them in my office from now on."

"Verrrry wise. They'll get seen by the right people then."

Their voices faded as they walked away towards

Lynette's office. A few minutes later Nicky heard their footsteps again, this time moving in different directions.

"Thanks for your help. I'll let you know if it works."

"It will. It never fails. Now I've got to rush. I've got a string of animals to get sorted out this morning." Melvyn's sloping strides disappeared back up the yard, and a moment later Nicky heard the whine of spinning tyres, before his car screamed away.

Nicky pushed his hands through his hair, trying to make sense of what he'd just heard. So at least it wasn't that lizard who was riding Puzzle, but he didn't feel a lot better for knowing that. What was that creep doing here at all, and what was Lynette up to with him?

Lynette's footsteps came hurrying back. "Oi, pack that in! You'll have the door down in a minute." Nicky heard a bolt sliding, and the heavy clatter of hooves as one of the horses followed her out. "OK then. Time to see what you can do today."

Keeping low, with Muffet purring and rubbing against his hand, Nicky peered round the corner. Puzzle was walking behind Lynette, and they were going through into the jumping field. Nicky couldn't make it out. She was on her own, and she hadn't even tacked him up. But surely she wasn't just taking him over to graze? The grass was always kept short in there, and sprinkled with sand. Puzzle could get colic if he tried to eat it. There were plenty of better fields if she was giving him some free time.

He strained to get a clearer view. They had reached the field. Puzzle was standing in the middle, his head dropped and his ears back slightly. Lynette was walking between the jumps, carrying the bundle she had taken from Melvyn. She began laying something brown across the poles.

On the grass a whip lay coiled like a thin black snake.

Suddenly she spun back, snatched up the whip, and cracked it behind Puzzle's heels. He jerked his head up, and began to canter round her in a slow circle. She cracked the whip again, moving in towards him. Puzzle stopped almost square, then turned and cantered the other way. Lynette waved him diagonally across the field, first one way, then the other.

Then she drove him towards the first jump. He went fast, racing at it almost sideways, and clearing it easily in his funny, lumpy way. He tried trotting back to the gate, but Lynette went towards him again, forcing him into a canter. Then she kept him moving round, going over the jump again – and again – and again.

Suddenly it all clicked into place. This was what Harjit Gopal had seen. This was what he had meant by Puzzle being "amazing to watch". Then another memory slid across his thoughts. Something Lynette had said when Nicky first started training Puzzle:

"I reckon if you put him in a field full of jumps with no rider on him at all, he'd still go over them happily."

How long had she been doing this? How much had Puzzle had to take? Nicky crept as near to the corner as he dared, keeping low.

Lynette raised the poles. They looked high. Higher than Nicky had ever seen Puzzle manage before.

And as she began to work him back towards the new jump, realization bit into Nicky so hard that he almost shouted out.

The odd brown shapes that were draped across the poles – he suddenly knew what they were. They were hedgehog skins, put there to catch on Puzzle's legs if he dared to brush against the jumps. Sharp enough to sting. Sharp enough to scare. But not sharp enough for the marks ever to show...

Muffet stared as Nicky sprang angrily out of the gap, his shoulder knocking against the web of the small brown spider. The silver threads trembled, the trapped beads of rain glittering with the movement. Muffet's eyes flicked sideways. Then she pounced, her sharp claws opening suddenly before the spider had a chance to scuttle away.

26

"What the hell are you doing to him?"

"There's nothing wrong with it. He wouldn't do it if he didn't want to." Lynette didn't look round, but cracked the whip again, this time taking Puzzle over the wall.

Puzzle cleared it, then trotted across, his ears pricked forward as he spotted Nicky. Nicky rubbed the mottled brown forehead, but kept his eyes on Lynette. "Don't give me that. Those hedgehog skins are cruel. You're scaring the hell out of him — frightening him into jumping higher."

"Don't be stupid. Loads of people use them. If we want to get him at top level, we've got to play top people's games."

Nicky strode towards the nearest jump, snatching

angrily at the hedgehog skins. The spikes pricked into his hand as he hurled them across the field. "What are you going to do next? What about an electric current through the poles? I'm sure your friend Melvyn could rig something up for you. Or maybe you could light petrol along the bottom of each jump. He'd be bound to leap a bit higher then."

Lynette's eyes slitted. "I like that one. A bit like jumping through burning hoops, or dancing on hot coals. You Gyppos do have some good ideas sometimes."

Nicky clenched his fists. His nails dug new scratches into his skin. His eyes sparked dangerously, but he battled to keep cool. He wasn't doing any good, going at her like this. If he wasn't careful, he was going to make things worse.

He turned back to Puzzle and stroked his neck. Puzzle pushed his nose into Nicky's shoulder. "But why do you need to do this? He's already working flat out. What more do you want from him?"

"I can't afford to risk having him as yesterday's news. If you want to get on in life, you've got to keep pushing."

"That's your philosophy, not his."

"You don't know that," Lynette's eyes narrowed again. "You think you're so switched on. You think you can talk to horses, but you don't really *know* what they're thinking, or what they want."

"I know horses don't jump fences like that because they feel like it. Left to themselves, most horses would just choose to graze the day away."

"Then that makes you as bad as me. I don't suppose horses would choose to be trained and ridden at all, but you're quite happy to do that to them. What I've been doing with Puzzle isn't wrong. It's just different."

Nicky felt the fury burn through him again. "So getting what you want through fear – like using those hedgehog skins – isn't wrong?"

"I bet it doesn't hurt any more than having some over-enthusiastic ten-year-old jabbing at your mouth on a Saturday morning. At least while Puzzle's our star jumper he doesn't have to put up with that."

"But it's your job to teach those ten-year-olds how *not* to jab mouths, not to go off and do something worse…"

"It's my *job*," Lynette said slowly, "to make sure this place makes a profit. If I don't do that, none of us gets anything anyway." She whirled the whip sharply above her head. Puzzle flinched and skittered sideways, snorting. Then she drove him back towards the jumps. As he took the first one his tail was flicking and he was drenched with sweat.

He turned towards the second, Lynette still driving hard behind him. He took it badly, slightly

140

off balance. As he landed, his back leg scraped the spiked pole. Nicky saw the shiver run through his whole body, and the hurt confusion cloud his eyes.

But it didn't stop Lynette. She pushed him towards the next one. He cleared it almost from standing, and with space to spare, but now his ears were laid right back and his eyes rolled with a new, wild fear. It wasn't just the pain that frightened him. The spiked brown skins still held the smell of death.

Nicky turned away, sickened.

Suddenly he heard a thud as something fell into the grass. His voice was low and shaking as he swung back to Lynette. "He's lost a shoe. You'll have to stop now."

Lynette pushed her hand through her hair irritably and let the whip drop to her side. Puzzle, still very frightened, understood the signal and walked over. Streams of water were running off him, and he was blowing hard. Although he stood beside Lynette, he wouldn't look at her, and kept staring away towards the woods.

Lynette snapped at Nicky, as if it was all his fault. "What a waste of a morning. I'll have to get John Clarke round now. I'll need to shoe him before Melvyn comes again tomorrow."

Nicky rubbed the backs of his hands into Puzzle, feeling tangles of tension in his shoulders and neck.

"What's he coming back for? Aren't we his biggest rivals? Aren't we the enemy?"

"He's interested."

"What in? Getting you to join him in his snake pit?"

"In buying Puzzle."

Nicky felt fear prickle the base of his spine. "But he's not for sale!"

Lynette gave a thin laugh. "All our horses are for sale, if the price is right."

"But – but to *Melvyn Leach*..."

Lynette grabbed hold of Puzzle's forelock, and began to lead him away. "Don't be so pathetic, Nicky. Puzzle can't possibly stay at the top of the tree for ever. If we sell him before the end of this season, while he's still at his peak, he'll have served his purpose with us."

"But Melvyn Leach is riddled with poison. Tom says there's been all sorts of scandals about him. Murdering hedgehogs is sick enough, but he's into horse doping, and bent dealing, and he was caught at a show once with tin tacks hidden in his horse's leg bandages – another warped way of making sure the horse doesn't hit the poles. He doesn't care what he stains his fingers with, as long as it gets him a profit."

Lynette shrugged. "You know what the newspapers are like. It might not all be true. And

142

anyway, Patty can't afford to wait. Puzzle's put our name on the map, but the prize money isn't exactly going to provide us with limousines over the winter."

Nicky was stung. Shocked. Disbelieving. "You can't mean *Patty* agrees with this?"

"Patty takes my advice. If it's what I want, then it's what she'll do."

"But what about Tom, and the deal she made me…"

"Oh, grow up, Nicky. Start living in the real world. Your 'arrangement' with Patty was stupid, and I've told her what I think about it."

"So…" Nicky's voice was hoarse. "Is she going back on her word? Isn't she going to let Tom stay there after all?"

"Like I said, Patty does what I say."

Nicky hung back, watching them go. He didn't trust himself to be near Lynette any more. And it wasn't just her he was disgusted with. He was even more revolted by himself. He'd used Puzzle too – to try and get something he wanted. It shouldn't have been up to Puzzle to try and save Tom, or Patty, or anyone else.

He would have been better to have refused to help Patty at the beginning. That Megan girl could have bought Puzzle. She would have been someone who really cared about him. She would have loved him for what he was, and not for what he could do for her.

A couple of times Puzzle whickered anxiously and tried to pull his head round to see if Nicky was following, but Lynette's grip was like a vice and he couldn't shake himself free.

At the gate, Lynette stopped suddenly. She turned, a thin smile twisting her lips. "Isn't it time you went back to school? Otherwise I might be forced to make a little phone call. Like to your headmaster, perhaps ... and maybe even a tiny visit to your dad this evening ... and of course, I may have to mention it to Patty. I don't think she'll be very keen on the idea of Mill Farm being a refuge for truants, do you?"

27

"Tom! Tom!" Nicky rattled the handle of the door to the bungalow, and peered in through the windows. Everything was silent. No buzz of chatter from the radio. No classical music playing quietly in the background.

The small kitchen window was half open. He could probably get through it with a bit of wriggling and squeezing. He climbed up on to the ledge and tried to wedge open the frame.

"Doing a bit of repair work?" Nicky froze, then let out a sigh of relief. It was Annie Hobbs, coming up the path.

He jumped back down on to the grass. "I was worried about Tom. The front door was locked."

"He's probably sleeping." Annie held up a key. "I

got this from Patty Lake last night. She's asked me to pop over and check the window frames and stuff – fix them up for the winter. She doesn't think Tom's up to doing it himself at the moment."

Nicky nodded, but didn't answer. This wasn't the right moment to tell Annie she could be wasting her time – if Lynette had her way, Tom wouldn't last out here till the autumn, let alone winter. "Are you going in?"

"I will do, once I've checked the outside. Patty told him I was coming, and he said it was OK for me to let myself in if he didn't answer the door. Do you want to wait, and we'll go together?"

Nicky shook his head. If he went in with Annie, it would be all small talk and stuff about the bungalow. He wouldn't get a chance to tell Tom what Lynette was up to. And on top of that, it wasn't fair to worry him. Getting him stressed wouldn't make him feel better.

"No, I'll get going. I only popped over to check that he was OK. If you're here, I don't need to worry."

Annie smiled. "Right – but Nicky—"

"What?"

"You ought to be careful. It's lucky that I know you, and trust you. If anybody else had seen you clambering about, you might have had the police swarming round here by now."

146

Nicky met her eyes. She was right. He was stupid to have even thought about trying to get in. It could all have blown up in his face. He knew she would never judge him because he was a Gypsy, but there was still plenty of people round here that might. Dad was always on about how they had to be more careful than anyone else, so that no one had an excuse to point the finger at them. He said getting seen by the gorgios doing anything odd or different was like shooting yourself in the foot.

He hesitated, about to ask her where Emily was, then suddenly realized she would be at school. School was a dangerous subject. "I'll have to go. I've got stuff to do."

Annie nodded. "Me too." She turned away, scraping at the paint in one corner of the window with a chisel.

Nicky left her, and set off across the soggy field towards the old mill. He wasn't quite sure where he was going, but he needed to stay away from the roads. The ground was boggy in places, and a couple of times he found himself up to his knees in mud. He'd have to tell Mum he'd been on a class nature trail or something.

He saw Maggie crouched among the reeds where the river met the mill. She was on her own – the other swans usually stayed further downstream, where the water was clearer. Maggie had her back to

Nicky, but she hissed warningly as he came near. Nicky wondered if swans could be worked with, like horses. Perhaps he could learn their language too. He stopped walking and hissed an answer at her. She shifted her body away from him, her fierce black eyes staring over towards the bungalow. Nicky suddenly remembered something Tom had once told him – that swans mate for life. Despite his dark mood, he grinned suddenly. So that was it! Tom was the only man she would ever listen to.

It started raining again, coming down in fine sheets. Nicky glanced round, looking for cover. He never minded the rain, but from the colour of the sky, this looked like it was settling in for some time.

The door to the water mill was half rotted. Nicky knew it was private, but it wasn't like he was going into somebody's home. And it was either that, or get drenched. He'd only sit in there till the rain stopped. He wouldn't go rooting about.

The whole place smelt musty, but was surprisingly dry. The roof had held up over the years, keeping the worst of the weather away. Nicky looked round slowly, his eyes growing accustomed to the shadowy dark.

The wooden floors, although uneven, seemed sound. Across the middle of the room ran an old line shaft. The cracked leather pulleys were still attached. Two huge circular stones lay at the back by the wall, and a rusted metal chain hung down from the ceiling. There were steps up to the next floor, but they didn't look safe enough to try.

From beneath the great wheel Nicky could hear water trickling. He peered down the shaft, but it was too dark to see. The grilles outside were silted up, so he guessed the river couldn't push through properly any more.

But the thing that really caught him were the cobwebs. They hung from the ceiling like decaying Christmas decorations. They stretched from the walls to drape ancient machines. They covered the windows like grey lace curtains pulled across to shut out the light.

Nicky walked to the nearest window, and tried to look out. He poked at the cobwebs, winding them on to a stick until they looked like dust-grey candyfloss. A Red Admiral butterfly appeared from nowhere and began battering itself against the glass. Nicky pushed on the rotted frame, struggling to force it open. It wouldn't move, so he stabbed at one corner with the stick. The soft wood crumbled suddenly and the pane broke away, landing with a thud on the grass outside. The butterfly hovered for a moment, sensing fresh air for the first time ever, then fluttered through.

Nicky sat on one of the giant stones. He wished he'd been able to speak to Tom and tell him what

Lynette was planning. But even as he thought it, he realized there was nothing much Tom could have said or done. He would have to save Puzzle on his own. But pleading with Lynette would be like pleading with a viper when you'd just trodden on its tail. And he couldn't risk talking to Patty. He'd probably only get her back up, and make things worse.

He wished there was a way to get Puzzle to jump badly, just for tomorrow when Melvyn Leach came to watch him. But Puzzle liked pleasing people. He'd do his best even if he was being made to jump over a crocodile with its jaws open. Nicky traced his fingers across the cold roughness of the stone. He had to think of something soon. By this time tomorrow, it could all be over. Melvyn Leach could be taking Puzzle away.

He sat for a long time, staring at nothing and listening to the scrabblings and scratchings in the gloom. He could hear birds moving about near the roof, and sometimes he picked out the tiny sounds of mice scuffling. This desolate place was probably a safe haven for hundreds of small creatures and insects.

At last the rain stopped. From the broken pane in the window, watery sunlight was seeping through. Nicky stepped outside. Everything smelt fresh and clean, and across the sky a rainbow stretched from behind the woods to somewhere beyond Tom's garden.

Nicky looked up at the pale yellow sun. It was mid-afternoon – school would be finishing. It was safe to be seen again. As Nicky squelched his way back home, an idea began to grow in him. It suddenly seemed so obvious, and so perfect for what he needed, that he didn't know why he hadn't thought of it before.

28

"I've got to go out soon. We're doing some local history stuff at school. I need to work on it this evening because I'll be at Mill Farm over the weekend. It's that county show a week from now, and I've got stacks to do." Nicky looked at Mum through the dressing table mirror, where she was brushing her hair.

"Remember we're eating at the 'Pig and Whistle' tonight. Will you come in when you've finished? You're bound to be hungry."

Nicky pulled a face. "I'll just get a pasty from the newsagent. I don't know how long I'll be." He tried to sound as vague as possible. Mum would be expecting him to be with Bretta – she helped him sometimes with homework – but he didn't want to drag her name into this if he could help it. He'd already used her once today.

"OK." Mum began twisting her hair into a plait. "It's just me and Dad then. Sabrina's gone into town with a couple of friends, and she's going back to watch a video with one of them afterwards. We'll pick her up on our way home."

Nicky nodded, only half listening. It was a bit early for what he was planning, but he wanted to get away from the trailer before Dad got back – he might have different ideas from Mum about how his son should spend the evening.

Mum was still changing as Nicky rummaged for a strong rope in the cupboard under one of the seats, and then left.

He walked quickly to the woods behind Mill Farm, shinned up a tree to sit amongst the damp mossy branches, and waited.

29

Puzzle moved restlessly round the shadowy stable, whickering softly and rubbing Nicky with his nose. Nicky touched him lightly on the forehead, and rubbed him back.

Outside, the yard was still and quiet. Lynette had gone home ages ago, and although the lights were on at the house, Nicky knew Patty almost never came down on her own in the evenings.

"Come on boy," he whispered softly, taking a halter from a hook on the wall. He slipped it over Puzzle's head. "It's time to go."

He slid the bolt on the stable door, then walked out quickly with Puzzle following obediently behind.

Only Muffet, creeping along the edge of the

154

stables, saw them go. He followed silently for a while, then slunk off amongst the trees as the rich smells of wood mice and voles called him away.

It was drizzling again, and the path through the woods was slippy. Nicky walked beside Puzzle, his fingers twisted into his mane, steadying him up on the slopes and turns. The darkness thickened. Trees bent across them. Shapes and shadows melted together, pulling the evening round them.

Nicky never minded the dark. He moved by instinct, and by feel, but Puzzle could sense different things. Sometimes he stopped, his ears pricked forward, blowing softly. Nicky knew there would be a fox, or maybe even a badger, nearby. Each time he rubbed Puzzle's forehead, whispering gently. After a moment Puzzle would walk on again.

By the time they reached the water mill the rain was pelting down.

Nicky led Puzzle round to the door, and waited as he stood at the entrance, sniffing cautiously. Nicky took one step through it, and stopped. Puzzle followed. Nicky took another step. Then another. Then another. At last they were in the dry.

He took the rope from inside his jacket and

knotted it on to Puzzle's halter. "I've got to do this," he said, tying it firmly to the steel pole of the line shaft. "I've got to know that you're safe."

Puzzle blew on him, then shook himself suddenly, sprays of water dancing off his coat and splattering Nicky.

"What's up?" Nicky laughed. "Don't you think I'm wet enough?" He hugged Puzzle quickly, then stepped back towards the door. "I won't be long," he promised. "I've just got to get a few bits and pieces."

He was back within five minutes, carrying one of the hay nets from Tom's shed, and some old sacks to rub Puzzle dry.

At last, when he was sure Puzzle was safe and comfortable, Nicky blew on his nose gently. "I know it's no five-star hotel," he whispered, "but we just have to sit this out through tomorrow, to give me a chance to chase up that Megan girl. Once she knows you're for sale, I'll get you back home again somehow. I just couldn't risk that reptile Melvyn getting you first." He pressed his lips softly against Puzzle's forehead, then slipped back out into the rain again.

He ran most of the way home, wondering whether there was a chance he could have got as wet as this just coming from Bretta's. But that was the least of his worries. As he squelched his way back across the site, Nicky saw the police car parked outside their trailer.

His insides twisted.

They were on to him already. They must have been waiting for him.

30

"She was lucky this time, Mr Ghiselli." Inspector Whymark, from Maybridge police station, was closing his notebook as Nicky slipped nervously in. "The shops were willing to let her go. But if it happens again…"

"What about the other two?" Dad's face was a thundercloud. "What's going to happen to them?"

"As I explained earlier, theirs is a slightly different situation. We … er … we have come up against them before, and the shops do tend to take a harder line in those circumstances. Shoplifting is a big problem these days, and they can't afford not to."

Inspector Whymark shook Dad's hand, nodded briefly at Nicky, and left.

Nicky didn't need to ask what was going on. The sight of Sabrina huddled and crying on the seat, Mum's face shocked and pale, and Dad's fist clenched and shaking, told him enough.

"So what have you got to say for yourself?" Sabrina shrank further into the cushions as Dad towered over her.

"Don't, Joseph. She's really been through it. She was even sick in that interview room. Can't you see she's had enough for one night?"

"*She's* had enough?! *She's* had enough!" Dad was bellowing, angry veins throbbing across his forehead.

Mum wedged herself in front of Sabrina.

Dad's voice dropped suddenly, low and dangerous. "Well, *I'm* only just about to begin."

"Leave it, Dad." Nicky spoke for the first time. "Give her a chance to think it all through."

Dad turned slowly, his anger moving on to Nicky. "Like she thought it through in the shopping precinct, you mean – when she let those *friends* persuade her to slip bits of make-up and jewellery in her pocket?"

Nicky held his gaze. At least while Dad was focused on him, he was giving Sabrina a break. "But you heard what Inspector Whymark said. It was her first time. The other two have probably been at it for years. They must have set Sabrina up—"

"No one ever 'sets anyone up' – unless that person lets them. All she had to do was say 'no' ."

"It's not easy sometimes, Dad. Not when everyone's going at you – because you're a 'Gyppo', because you can't read, because you don't fit—"

"Do you think it's easy for me, grovelling to the likes of that Anderson woman that teaches her, or that scorpion Lynette at Mill Farm? Do you think I don't hear the slant in their voices? Do you think I don't see the way they look at me? It's a hard enough job, trying to carve out a good name for this family, and your sister could have just smashed it away for a pocketful of glittery face paint."

"You brought us here. You said you wanted us to settle in one place…"

"Don't swing that one at me again. You know it was just as rough travelling around. Life was never meant to be easy, and I'm just trying to do my best."

Dad's fist jerked suddenly. Nicky wondered if he was about to get a clout. They glared at each other.

Then Dad dropped his eyes. "I'm going out," he growled. "I want some space from here…"

He pushed past Nicky towards the door, and a moment later they heard the pick-up start, and go roaring away.

Nicky closed his eyes, slumping downwards into the seat. He was wet through, and suddenly realized he was shivering.

"I'll get you a hot drink." Mum put her hand on his shoulder as she walked past. "I think we could all do with something."

Nicky didn't answer. Now that Dad had gone, he had a chance to think straight. If this was what happened when Sabrina stole some make-up, what the hell would Dad do if he knew Nicky had stolen a horse?

31

Nicky went back to Jim's trailer to get dry clothes.

Jim, who'd been keeping his head down while the police were round, was still awake. "What were the gavvers doing here?" he asked.

"For Sabrina. Shoplifting." Nicky rummaged through the drawer under the seat. In times of trouble Gypsies always close in together, but he felt like a creep even telling Jim about it.

Jim whistled through his teeth. "He's got a giant temper, your dad. But he'll calm down. He'll get things back to size again."

Nicky nodded, pulling on clean jeans and a sea-green sweatshirt. "Maybe."

But he wasn't too sure. And Jim didn't know

what Nicky knew. Jim didn't know that Nicky had spent the evening doing something worse.

He walked back to the other trailer. It was very late, but there wasn't much point going to bed. He would never have slept.

Mum, her eyes heavy and hollow, kept yawning.

"You get some sleep," Nicky said at last. "I'll sit with her."

Mum hesitated. "I don't think..."

"Look, it's stupid for us both to be here. And you'll have Dad to face in the morning." He gave her a short smile. "You'll need all your strength for that."

Mum smiled weakly back. "*If* he comes back..."

"Course he will. Whatever else he does, he wouldn't leave you."

Sabrina stayed huddled for a long time, and refused to talk. Nicky sat with her, making hot drinks that went cold, or just holding her hand.

"You must really hate me," she sniffed between sobs at last. "If this gets out things'll be miserable for you as well as for me."

Nicky squeezed her fingers. "We all do stupid things that seem right at the time..."

"But that's just it. It *didn't* feel right at the time. I knew it was stupid even then. I was just too pathetic to stand up for myself. And that policeman was wrong. I had done it before – just once. I nicked

163

some lipstick for Kelly's birthday present. I didn't have any money to buy her anything, and I wanted her to like me…" Slow tears rolled down her face again.

Nicky stared past her towards the window. The clouds had thinned, and a fine thread of moonlight stole in through a gap in the curtains. He glanced down at Sabrina. She was swaying with tiredness, sitting half-upright in the seat. Nicky pulled a blanket over her, then sat listening as her breathing grew even and deep. If Sabrina was stupid and pathetic, what did that make him?

He ran through it endlessly, twisting it over and over in his mind, until a hazy pink dawn began to soak through the darkness outside.

Very quietly, he got up.

Then, creeping softly, he tiptoed his way out of the trailer. Lynette never got to Mill Farm before seven-thirty. There was still time to get Puzzle back without anyone ever knowing he'd been gone. And there were other ways to deal with the problem. He'd talk to Patty. Make sure she understood about Melvyn Leach. Make her see she must never sell Puzzle to him.

He was wiping the rain from the saddle on his bike when Dad came back. He got out of the pick-up, crumpled and unshaven. Nicky looked up, prepared for the next explosion. It didn't come.

"It looks like everybody's at it."

"At what?"

"It's your mate Tom now."

"Why? What's happened?" A finger of unease ran down Nicky's back.

"I've just been over there. I'd been driving round, putting off coming home."

"Go on."

"Of course, it proves a point. The bloke must be senile."

"Is Tom hurt, Dad? Is he all right?"

"I mean ... I don't reckon it could have been an act of revenge. He wouldn't have been that stupid..."

"What is it, Dad? What's happened to Tom?"

"He's nicked that horse, that's what. The one that you ride. I saw them all over there – Lynette and Patty Lake putting the animal in a horse-box, and the whole place crawling with gavvers. I reckon—"

Nicky didn't wait to hear any more. "I've got to go. I've got to try and sort it out."

"Hey! Hold on! Don't get involved. It's gorgios' stuff. It's nothing to do with you..." Dad stepped forward to grab at his handlebars, but Nicky swerved round him and hurtled off across the site, skidding and sliding through every dip and hump in the ground on the way.

32

"I'm here about Tom Hughes. He didn't do it."

Sergeant Simms raised his eyebrows as Nicky burst into the reception area of Maybridge Police Station. "It's Nicky, isn't it? Nicky Ghiselli? We've had you in before."

"It was different last time. It wasn't my fault."

"And this time it is?"

Nicky's throat went dry as he remembered his last scrape with the police, when he was suspected of spraying graffiti on to horses. The memory of being locked in the cell, with its tiny glass-brick window and stink of urine, still made him feel sick when he thought about it. Now he was about to put himself through the whole thing again.

Sergeant Simms glanced round as a police-woman, typing something into a computer, handed him a sheet of paper. He frowned. "I've got your name here already. Weren't you in yesterday evening?"

"That was my sister. About something else."

Sergeant Simms ran a weary hand across his stubbled chin. "I see. Nothing like a bit of family continuity, I suppose. So what can we do for you?"

Nicky hesitated, and pushed his hands into his jeans pockets. There was a packet of gum in one of them, and he began to pick at the foil wrapper with his fingernails. "You've got to let Tom Hughes go. He's an old man, and he's not well. You can't keep him locked up in here."

"And why would we want to lock Tom Hughes up in the first place?"

"Because you think he stole Puzzle – Patty Lake's horse. But he didn't. It was me."

Sergeant Simms' expression changed suddenly, like someone who'd just discovered the kitten on their lap was really a tiger. "OK, Nicky. We'd better get hold of your parents, and then I'll take a proper statement…"

The policewoman led Nicky through the long corridors to the cells. "Please remove your laces. You can leave them outside the door."

Nicky fumbled, pulling them out through the

holes, then dropped them into a sad grey huddle on the floor.

The policewoman took a giant silver key from the belt round her waist, and unlocked the door. Nicky followed her inside the cell. His hands were sticky with sweat and he was already shaking.

The door slammed shut.

Nicky paced the cell like a caged animal, watching his feet, listening to the echoes of sound from the corridor outside. He tried not to think about the stark white walls, or the tiny window that could never open. He knew he was doing the right thing. He could never live with himself, letting Tom take the rap for something he hadn't done.

But as the thoughts kept buzzing, he wasn't sure if it was being trapped in the cell, or the thought of what Dad was going to say, that was scaring him most.

Nicky's heart twisted when Mum came in. She looked small, very frail, her face still blotched and strained from last night. "Lucky your dad went out logging this morning," was all she said.

Nicky picked at the frayed cuff of his sweatshirt, and didn't answer.

Sergeant Simms began to speak. "This interview is being tape-recorded. I am PC 1471 Simms. The other adult present is Mrs Kathleen Ghiselli. I am interviewing Nicky Ghiselli…" He finished the formal announcement and leaned back in his seat, locking his fingers together across his chest. "So – what exactly do you want to say?"

"It wasn't Tom who took Puzzle. I took him and hid him in the old water mill because I thought … well, because…" Nicky shrugged, hunching forward in his chair and staring at a watery stain on the brown cord carpet. The whole room held the sharp tang of disinfectant. He wondered if it was where Sabrina had thrown up earlier.

"Go on."

"It wasn't like proper stealing. I wasn't going to sell him or anything. I would've taken him back."

"So why did you take him in the first place?"

Nicky looked up suddenly. "Because Lynette was going to sell him to Melvyn Leach. I had to try and stop her."

Sergeant Simms cracked his knuckles and considered Nicky for a moment. "I thought the horse belonged to Patty Lake?"

"He does, but she's just a sort of puppet. She does what Lynette says."

"And why would stealing the horse for a couple of days help? If Melvyn Leach really wanted him, he could just buy him next weekend instead of this, couldn't he?"

Nicky looked away again. Sergeant Simms was right. It all seemed so pathetic now.

Sergeant Simms stifled a yawn. He'd been working all night, and he was ready to go home. "You could end up in the Youth Court. Your parents could get fined. You might wind up at an Attendance Centre. You'll get a police record. And then there's the cruelty charges…"

Nicky's head jerked round. "I wasn't cruel. I made sure he was safe."

"That old mill's rotted through in places. Suppose your horse put his great hoof on the wrong plank? Or suppose a bit of the roof caved in when you weren't there?"

"But I'd checked it all out earlier. I knew it was all right."

"Premeditated, eh? And that brings me to something else – the small matter of trespass. That mill is a privately owned building, on private land."

"OK. I know. It was a stupid thing to do."

"A very stupid thing."

Nicky let his head drop. He rubbed his hand across his eyes. He was achingly tired. He wanted all this over with. He wanted Sergeant Simms to stop piling more and more muck on top of him. As long as they let Tom out, they could chuck him back in the cell now, for all he cared. He spoke in a dead, flat voice. "So will you let Tom go?"

Sergeant Simms leaned forward in his chair

suddenly. "What would you say if I told you Tom Hughes wasn't actually here?"

Startled, Nicky looked up. "Where have you taken him?"

Sergeant Simms gave a funny, sorry sort of smile. "Nowhere. We never arrested him in the first place."

"But my dad said he saw—"

"Your dad probably put two and two together and made five." This time Sergeant Simms did yawn, stretching his mouth wide open and showing silver fillings in his back teeth. "There was a lot going on at that water mill this morning. Old Tom came out in his pyjamas when we knocked him up just after six. Nobody thought for one minute that he had anything to do with it."

"So – what did they think?" Nicky didn't feel tired any more. Just sick.

"The blonde one – Lynette – wanted to make a statement but Patty Lake wouldn't let her. She said she'd sort it out in her own way." Sergeant Simms gave Nicky a hard look. "I don't think she was having her strings pulled then, do you?"

Nicky put his hands over his eyes, as if shutting out Sergeant Simms could somehow shut everything else out too. It didn't work. Thoughts spat and cracked through his mind like fireworks across the sky. He should have checked Tom's place first. He should have gone to see Patty. He should have faced up to Lynette.

"Come on," Sergeant Simms said softly. "We've got your statement, and we'll drive you both home. Then we'll contact Patty Lake again, and see what action she intends to take once she knows you've been in to see us."

Nicky got up slowly. It had all been for nothing. And if Patty decided to take things further after all, he'd have dropped himself right in it – or, as Dad would say, he'd have shot himself in the foot.

But thinking about Dad set off a new panic.

Dad wouldn't be bothered about Nicky shooting himself in the foot – he'd be too busy aiming his own gun at Nicky's head.

33

"Get over to Jim's trailer!" Dad pointed at Mum and Sabrina.

"Joseph … I…"

"Just get round there. I'm not going to hurt him, I just want him on his own."

Mum shot Nicky a helpless look, then ushered Sabrina out.

Nicky got up slowly and stood to face Dad.

The explosion came straight away. "A horse thief!" he roared. "That's what everyone will say. That's the label you've gone and stuck on yourself."

"It wasn't like that—"

"Do you think anyone's going to care *why* you did it? Do you think anyone's going to listen?" Dad was spitting as he spoke. His eyes burned dark and dangerous.

Nicky tried to hold Dad's stare. "Maybe no one will find out…"

"And maybe pigs will fly!" Dad slammed his fist hard on to the kitchen work top. Mum's best fine bone china rattled in the display cabinet above. "And even if it never goes any further, enough people know already. And one day, when it suits them, one of them might decide to use it against you." Dad shook his head and whistled out through his teeth.

"But it wasn't proper stealing. I told the gavvers—"

"I don't care what story you spun for the gavvers. They've got you on their books now – twice. What with you and your sister – between you you're destroying us all." Dad grabbed a plate from the rack and hurled it suddenly across the trailer. It hit the wall, smashing into four jagged pieces.

He kept his eyes locked on to Nicky, as new monsters seemed to wake and rush into his mind. "And horse theft isn't the only thing you've been up to," he roared suddenly. "What makes me sicker than anything is the way you've been going behind my back. That deal with the Lake woman. She told me about it this morning – when I went to see her after you cycled off like a lunatic."

Nicky swallowed hard, "I … I didn't know you'd gone there."

"I only wanted to find out what I could about Tom for you. But what she told me made my blood boil. You *knew* I was waiting on that land clearance work coming in, but you hatched up a plan with her that might mean it never comes off!"

"It just seemed like – like if I didn't do something, I was letting Tom down."

Dad began to pace the length of the trailer. "So you let us down instead. Your own family. Mum, Jim and I are working ourselves to shreds trying to build a living here, but that's not important to you, is it? It's good to know where your loyalties lie."

"It wasn't like that. I didn't think—"

"You're damn right you didn't." Dad stopped pacing and strode over to Nicky. He raised his fist, and pushed it close to Nicky's face.

Nicky moved back. His eyes stayed locked with Dad's, but his throat felt full of stones, and the race of his heart thundered in his head.

Suddenly Dad let his hand drop back to his side. His voice went flat, tired and empty. "You'd better get on and help your mother. I don't care what you do any more. I've got a job to get to, and I'm already late."

Mum and Sabrina crept back in as the pick-up skidded away. They quietly got out cloths, and polish, and cleaning things. Nicky swept up the broken plate, and checked through the cabinet of bone china. Two of the fine-edged tea cups were cracked. He wrapped them all in plastic bags, sellotaping them carefully, as if they were gifts. They each worked silently, as if they'd made some sort of unspoken pact.

"Is it OK if I go out for a while?" Sabrina said at last. "I've got some drawing to do for homework."

Mum squeezed her shoulders. "Make sure you're back by lunch."

Both of them had blotched, swollen faces, looking like they'd fallen head-first into a clump of stinging nettles.

Nicky went outside and dug a hole round the back of the trailer. He dropped the bags in the soft dark spaces, then filled them in again.

When he was finished, he sat beside Sky on the lorry tyre, and combed great balls of hair out of her coat.

Mum came out and sat beside him.

Nicky pulled a tangle of fur from the comb. "So how come you're not going loopy too?"

"Bits of me are. Bits of me want to shake you both. Bits of me want to shout and break things like Dad did. It's tough for me too, living here. I get nasty remarks sometimes, the same as the rest of you. All of this just gives people more muck to sling

176

at us." She sighed, reaching forward to rub Sky's ears. "But…"

"But what?"

"I guess the other bits of me feel guilty. Me and Dad have been so busy. In the old days I was always home for you, but sometimes now I'm not even around when you get in from school. I've been relying on Jim looking out for you. But perhaps if I'd been here more…"

Nicky shrugged. "For Sabrina maybe, but not for me. I don't think anything would have stopped me." He turned to Mum awkwardly. "I'm sorry I've made such a mess of everything."

Sky rolled over as Nicky stopped combing, sticking her legs in the air. Absently Mum began tickling her tummy. "I suppose you were following your heart. I can't really be angry with you for that…"

They looked up as a tatty blue car bounced towards them across the site.

Nicky turned to Mum and drew an imaginary slit across his throat. "It's Patty Lake. It looks like I'm about to hear my sentence."

"Do you want me to talk to her?"

Nicky shook his head. "It's OK. It's my problem. I'll sort it out."

Mum pulled a face, then nudged Nicky. "I'll go and make some tea. Call me if you need me."

Patty got out of her car and walked over. She stopped just in front of Nicky, chewing the tip of her little finger. "I just wanted to let you know, I've spoken to the police, but I'm still not planning to press charges. If anything, I'm impressed that you had the guts to go into the station like that."

Nicky kicked at the ground, working a flat grey stone out from the mud with the edge of his trainer. It felt awkward, having her here like this. "Thanks."

"That doesn't mean I'm happy with what you did. You gave us all a fright this morning. Me, Tom and Lynette. You did something stupid, and it could have been dangerous too." She sighed, breaking her split nail off and flicking it into the grass. "But you've worked well for me this last month or so. I'm willing to leave it at that."

"Is Lynette happy with that?"

"I make my own decisions. And when she told me about Melvyn Leach wanting to get his claws on Puzzle, I guessed what had been in your head." Her voice softened suddenly. "I did understand."

Nicky hesitated, and looked up at her. "So how did you find out where Puzzle was?"

"Lynette came in early because she had the blacksmith coming. She did a quick scout round as soon as she discovered he was missing. There were hoof prints leading into the wood – only three out of four prints were shod," Patty shook her head.

"She said you may as well have hung signs up saying *This Way To Puzzle*."

"So is he OK?"

"You know Puzzle. He takes things in his stride."

"That's just the trouble though, isn't it? That's how we've all got away with using him like this." Nicky bent to pick up the stone and turned it between his fingers, scratching off bits of soft, clinging moss.

Patty sighed. "I know it must seem like that at the moment, but he's a great horse. I'm really fond of him. I would never do anything to hurt him."

"So you're definitely keeping him then?"

"I will if I can. He's made a big difference to us, and he's brought us lots of new customers. But you have to understand … there's a chance I might have to sell all of the horses if that doesn't keep up."

"So if I keep jumping him for you, it's for his own sake now? It's to make sure you can afford to keep him?"

Patty knelt down to stroke Sky, avoiding Nicky's eyes. "I'm sorry, Nicky. Your Dad's banned you from riding. Or that's what he told me this morning. I thought he would have told you too."

Nicky stared at her, then skimmed the stone suddenly across the site. It landed with a dull rattle against an old oil drum. Then he pushed his hands roughly through his hair, shaking his head angrily.

When it came to punishments with him and horses, Dad always knew exactly where to aim.

"Tea's ready!" Mum opened the trailer window and leaned out.

Nicky tried to keep his voice level as he led Patty inside. "So how can Puzzle keep winning if you haven't got anyone to ride him?"

"Lynette's going to do it. She said she's still got a week to practise, and she's determined to get the hang of him." Patty smiled round the room as Mum handed her the tea in one of the bone china cups. "What a lovely home. It all looks so clean and fresh. I wish I had time to keep my place together like this."

34

"You've got to go. I need you there." Dad sprinkled grated cheese over his spaghetti and took a swig of beer. "Annie Hobbs wants help on her stall. I've told her we'll both be around."

Nicky closed his eyes. However much he liked Annie and Emily, having to be cheerful to a load of gorgios while Lynette was smarming about nearby on Puzzle was the last thing he wanted to deal with. He'd heard that she was definitely riding him – Bretta had bumped into her a few days before, and she'd been full of smug comments about "how easy Puzzle was to ride, now she'd had a proper chance to get used to him."

He pushed his food round his plate with his fork. It suddenly tasted like rubber.

"You'll be all right," Mum said gently, as if she was reading his thoughts. "You'll have to face up to Lynette some time. You may as well get it over with."

"I'll be there anyway," Sabrina cut in. "Miss Anderson from school says I've got to go. I brought home a letter about it. Don't you remember, Dad? I gave it to you on Wednesday."

Dad got another beer from the fridge. Sabrina had been banned from going anywhere, but a letter from school was different. "We'll all go then."

"Sounds good," Jim said slowly. "You go off and enjoy yourselves. I'll stay back and mind the trailers."

"I don't know about 'enjoy'," Dad grunted darkly, snapping off the ring pull. "We're not going there for that. And we'll be keeping a strict eye on you two. And if either of you gets into any more trouble…"

Nicky let his fork fall on to his plate with a clatter. All this week he'd felt trapped, as if Dad had him tied up on invisible rope – dragging him round places that he didn't want to go, and keeping him away from all the places that he did.

The trailer never felt smaller. The site never looked filthier.

It had almost seemed like a treat, just being able to go to school.

He got up suddenly, going outside and slamming the door. Sky came over to him, her ears down and her tail wagging uncertainly. Nicky sat on the lorry tyre and put his arms round her, pulling her to him tightly.

It was killing him, not being able to go over and take care of Puzzle. And if Lynette was training as hard as Nicky was imagining, the chances were it was killing Puzzle too.

35

Annie's stall was squeezed between a needle-thin woman giving lacemaking demonstrations, and the hot dog van.

In the ring opposite a collection of gleaming old fashioned steam rollers paraded lazily round. Nearby a clown was selling balloons.

Across the field, on the far side, was the horse show. Nicky could hear the muffled announcements over the loudspeaker, and see the occasional competitor browsing amongst the stands. Someone came and fingered Annie's carved animals, and then splashed out on a napkin ring.

"Are you riding Puzzle after you've helped us?"

Emily, who'd been busy exploring while they were setting up, came back munching a hot dog.

Nicky knelt down to her level. "It's a long story."

"I like stories." Emily wiped a splodge of tomato sauce off her chin. "Has it got a happy ending?"

"It's one of those modern ones like you see on telly – the sort where Cinderella doesn't go to the ball."

Emily regarded him with wide hazel eyes. "Was she upset?"

"Very."

Annie looked up from chiselling the horn of a sandalwood unicorn, and gave Emily a sharp look. "Not so many questions, young lady. And how did you get that hot dog?"

"Bill gave it to me. He said I looked like I needed fattening up."

Annie raised her eyebrows and shrugged at Nicky. "She knows more people than I do at these places. We've been to so many shows this summer, and she's charming her way round everyone." She raised her thumb and made a sign towards the cheery-faced man in the hot dog van. The man grinned and waved back.

Suddenly Nicky spotted two girls hurrying past, giggling. It was Kelly and Carla.

"Can I nip off for a moment?"

Annie dug in her pocket for a tissue to wipe Emily's fingers. "No problem. You've been great this morning. You deserve a break."

"Cheers." Nicky darted through the crowd after them. He didn't know why he was following them, or what he was going to say, but he suddenly wanted to take the grins off their faces. Sabrina had been dragged off somewhere with Mum and Dad, and he couldn't imagine *she* was doing much giggling.

They were a little way ahead, and he had to dodge between buggies, and dogs, and people chattering in cheerful huddles. He kept them in sight by fixing on Carla's bright yellow T-shirt, and the pink spotted ribbon in Kelly's bobbing pony tail.

Up ahead was a huge marquee, and Nicky saw the girls disappear inside.

It was stiflingly hot. Nicky was wearing white jeans and a short-sleeved T-shirt, but he was still sweating. The marquee was squashed full of people, all craning their necks towards the far end. Nicky began scanning the faces for Carla and Kelly – and then stopped.

A film crew were there, with spotlights and cameras. In the centre of the set was Aileen Forbes from *Crazy About Creatures*. Talking to her – her face glowing with excitement – was Sabrina.

Moving sideways, Nicky pushed and elbowed his way to the front.

As he got closer, he could see Aileen Forbes holding something up. It was a poster showing a bird of some sort, and Nicky suddenly realized it was a picture of Maggie. Her broken wing jutted out awkwardly, but the white of her feathers seemed lit with a magical light, standing out against the gloom of the derelict mill. Along the top, in glittery gold lettering, were the letters SOS, and underneath Nicky could work out the three words *Save Our Swans*.

"It looks great, doesn't it? I wish I could do things like that."

Feeling a nudge on his elbow, Nicky glanced round to see Jade standing beside him. Her usually pale face was flushed from being dressed in jodhpurs and jacket in the baking marquee. He grinned at her. "That's my sister they're talking to. It was a school project."

Jade squinted and put her head on one side. "She looks a bit like you. What school does she go to?"

"Maybridge School. The same as me."

Jade's smile lit up her face. "I'm going there, next term. Mum thinks the private school isn't doing me any good, and I've got to move. I've been really worried about not knowing anyone."

"Hang around, and I'll get you to meet Sabrina — if she ever comes down to earth again." Catching sight of Mum and Dad, Nicky grabbed Jade's elbow and edged his way across to them.

"It's a beautiful poster, Sabrina. A very worthy winner. What gave you the idea for it?" Aileen

Forbes flashed rows of immaculate teeth, and nodded encouragingly as she spoke.

"My brother told me about it. He's got a friend who lives near there, and he rescued the swan when she nearly died getting caught up on the power lines. Tom – my brother's friend – says all the council have to do is put silver balls along the lines so the swans can see them. But they won't do it, and my brother told me swans – and other birds – die every year because of it…"

Mum raised her eyebrows and smiled as Nicky drew level, and even Dad grunted a greeting.

"When did she do that?" Nicky whispered to Mum.

"Last weekend, I think. When she went out sketching. But I didn't know—"

"It was probably what that letter was about. The one she gave Dad from school. Pity he couldn't read it – we might all have had an easier week if he had."

Mum nodded, then sighed. "Still, you know what your dad's like. He'd rather chuck something in the bin than let on he couldn't work out what it said…"

The camera swung back to focus again on Aileen Forbes. Her teeth glinted into the lens. "Well, you'll be glad to know that everyone in the *Crazy About Creatures* team is *fascinated* by the story Sabrina's been telling us. Watch us on Channel Three next week, when we plan to follow it up with a visit to the mill."

In the background the *Crazy About Creatures* theme tune began to play. The camera closed in close on Sabrina. Aileen Forbes leant forward and whispered something to her, and she giggled.

Nicky touched Mum's arm. "This is Jade. She's starting at our school next term and I thought it would be nice if she met Sabrina."

Mum smiled and nodded warmly as Nicky turned to Jade. "D'you mind if I leave you with my mum? I've got to get back to the stall I'm helping on. Tell Sabrina she was brilliant."

As he pushed his way back through the crowd, Nicky stopped and looked round once more. Sabrina's interview was finished, and she had already hurried over to the others. Mum was hugging her, Dad was giving her a quick pat on the back, and Jade was hovering shyly just behind them. As he watched, he saw Mum take Jade's arm. Jade stepped forward and smiled at Sabrina. Sabrina smiled back.

As Nicky turned away again, he suddenly caught sight of a flash of yellow and dotted pink. Kelly and Carla were weaving their way back through the marquee ahead of him. They weren't giggling any more.

When they got outside and turned right, Nicky didn't bother to follow them.

36

Nicky was just selling his tenth napkin ring of the day when Dad came over.

"How's it going?"

"He's doing a grand job." Annie began to smooth the unicorn's legs with sandpaper. "We've had a busy morning so far."

"Good lad." Dad grunted in Nicky's direction, and picked up one of the painted pine toilet roll holders. "Do you sell many of these?"

"Women seem to like them," Annie Hobbs grinned. "They'll all be sold by the end of the day."

Dad winked at Nicky, and put the holder back down. "Well – no offence meant, but if Mum comes over, tell her you've sold out. Tell her all these are for display purposes only."

Nicky suddenly felt another tug at his elbow. "Nicky! Nicky! You've got to come. I've just seen Puzzle and he looks all funny."

Nicky looked down at Emily, who was hopping from one foot to the other. "What are you talking about?"

"Puzzle. There's a lady with him who keeps shouting, and a horrid man with a whip, but Puzzle won't take any notice of either of them. He just looks … broken."

Nicky turned to Dad and Annie. "I've got to go. I've got to find out what's going on."

Annie walked round the front of the stall, squeezed Nicky's arm and hugged Emily. "Both of you go. You'll be quicker if Emily takes you straight to him."

Dad nodded. "I'll stay and help Annie. Oh – and Nicky…"

"Yes?"

"If there's really something wrong with the horse – if there's any way you can help – you must do whatever you can."

Their eyes met for a moment, then Nicky nodded. "Sure." Then, grabbing Emily's hand, the two of them began to run across the field towards the horse show.

37

Even from a distance, Nicky could see Puzzle looked all wrong.

He was standing by the practice jump, his head drooping and his whole body hunched and strange.

But it wasn't just that. Nicky squinted, trying to make sense of it. There seemed to be a shadow across him, and his outline was fuzzy and uncertain – as if he was tangled in cobwebs. Nicky suddenly realized he was seeing something nobody else could see. He wasn't just seeing a tired, washed-out horse. He was seeing Puzzle's exhaustion and pain.

Nicky dropped Emily's hand, and sprinted the last hundred metres to reach him.

Lynette stepped back. "I wondered if you'd show

up." Her voice was shaky, and for once she didn't seem sorry to see him.

"How long has he been like this?"

"It's just happened now. He was fine yesterday. We had some reporters over, and he was jumping for them. He was loving it."

Nicky touched Puzzle gently. Close up, he could see sludge-grey colours hanging over the horse's shoulders and neck. Darts of violent red were vibrating across his head. A dirty sea-green washed his belly and legs, and his hooves were tainted with dull aching yellow. Nicky had seen colours on horses before, right from when he was little. They showed him when a horse was sick, and depressed. But until now, he'd never seen so many, or so clear.

"Can you do anything? He's supposed to be jumping in ten minutes."

Nicky wheeled round on her. "You surely can't still be planning to enter him!"

"They're all waiting for him. He's the highlight of the event. That *Crazy About Creatures* crew are planning to film him. It's exactly what we've been working for—"

"What *you've* been working for!" Nicky snapped.

"And you, Nicky," Lynette said softly. "It was you that made that deal with Patty."

"Stuff Patty. And stuff the deal. If I get Puzzle better, it'll be for himself, not for anybody else!"

He reached up to touch Puzzle's forehead, and felt a stinging pain buzz through his fingers. He leaned his head against Puzzle's nose. He couldn't bear it, to think that he had been part of this.

"I've brought the trailer over if you need to get him inside." Patty arrived suddenly, her face criss-crossed with worry. "And I've called a vet. She's busy with a mare and foal at the moment, but she shouldn't be too long."

Around them a small crowd was gathering. Other competitors had tied their horses up and hurried over to help, or to stare. There was a frightened silence. Emily started to cry.

Bretta hurried across. "What do you think's happened to him?"

"Over-jumped, probably. It happens sometimes. I've seen horses like this before. It's a kind of shutting down."

As he spoke, Nicky noticed Jade hovering anxiously in the background. She came closer, her face paler than ever. "Can I help?"

Puzzle seemed to be swaying, and for a moment Nicky thought he was actually going to fall. "Hold his head," he said to her suddenly. "And Bretta — can you get his saddle off, very gently? I'm going to try working on him."

Nicky had healed horses before, but never in public. Never before a crowd. Grandad used to tell

194

him it was a secret gift. Something to keep private, and special. But here, at the show, there was nowhere private to go, and he wouldn't leave Puzzle like this. He would just have to do his best.

Nicky walked all round Puzzle, running his fingers gently along his spine. Sometimes, as he touched, his fingers jabbed, like a sudden jolt of electricity was passing through. He ran his hands over Puzzle's whole body, his eyes half-closed, sensing the parts that were locked up, or painful. And when he felt the knots Nicky pressed more firmly, stroking in tight circles, feeling the centres of pain dissolve into tiny fragments that washed away with the new flows of energy that were breaking through.

Nicky forgot where he was. He forgot the crowd. He forgot the show. He became part of Puzzle, blending with him, melting against him, his own strength passing into him like a fast-flowing stream bubbling through a tired brown river.

The change came slowly. Nicky felt Puzzle stand straighter. He sensed him raise his head. He heard the friendly, familiar snort as Puzzle seemed to wake up and begin to look round. Then there came a nudge in his back. Jade had let go of his head, and Puzzle was nibbling the collar of Nicky's shirt.

There was a ragged cheer from the small audience. A few people came up and touched

Nicky's arm. "That was wonderful." "Impressive stuff." "I didn't think it would work – perhaps you could come over to my stable one day."

Even Melvyn Leach, watching on Bullet over by the practice jump, flicked him a thumbs-up sign before cantering away.

Lynette grabbed Puzzle's saddle and began to put it back on him. "They're calling him, Nicky. It's Puzzle's turn to jump."

Nicky stared at her in disbelief, "You *can't* mean to ride him. Even you can't be that cruel."

"The film crew are there," she hissed. "We have to perform."

"This isn't a circus."

"But he's better. Look at him. You've sorted him out."

Nicky turned to Patty, who was twisting her fingers through Puzzle's mane. "You could finish him off if you push him again so soon."

Around the ring the crowd, wondering where the newest star of show jumping had got to, were beginning to chant, *"Puzzle! Puzzle! Puzzle!"*

Patty turned to Lynette. "Of course you can't ride him," she said firmly. "If he suddenly collapses, what good would that do any of us? But..." she turned back to Nicky. "Maybe you could just walk him round. Let everyone see he's OK. Explain to the judges he's been a bit off colour..."

Nicky looked at Puzzle. He was standing tall, his ears pricked, looking towards the jumps and the chanting crowd. "Just one circuit then. Very, very gently."

Patty produced a hat, a jacket, and even boots in Nicky's size from the bag of spares she kept in the trailer. There wasn't time for anything else. "You'll probably get away with the white jeans, just this time," she whispered.

The announcer was doing one last call as Nicky trotted Puzzle through into the ring.

38

A cheer broke out as they arrived. People called Puzzle's name. Cameras were clicking. Over on the far side, Nicky could see the television crew starting to film. Puzzle nodded his head as they walked round, blowing softly, as if he was calling out greetings. He was moving easily, happy and relaxed. He seemed to be coping.

"Maybe we could go wild and trot," Nicky murmured. "Just as we go over to tell the judges what we're up to."

Puzzle gave a long snort and flicked his ears.

The judges were sitting on benches under a covered stand, and Nicky turned Puzzle towards them. It probably wasn't going to go down well, telling them that Puzzle wouldn't be jumping after all. And he was sorry to be letting down Aileen Forbes and her team too, but it couldn't be helped. There was no way he was going to take any risks with Puzzle today.

Puzzle trotted briskly, tossing his head and lifting his feet high. People leaned against the rope, stretching their arms out and calling to him. Delighted, Puzzle gave his funny, prancing little dance and flicked his tail.

"Show off," Nicky whispered. "What d'you think this is? Auditions for *Son of Black Beauty* or something?"

They were getting close to the judges, and the beginning of the course.

Suddenly Puzzle broke into a canter, twisting his body so that he was moving sideways. Nicky battled to steer him back, pulling his head round sharply, but Puzzle was too strong. He fought against the bit, lowered his head, and aimed himself at the first jump.

"You stubborn old fool," Nicky muttered between gritted teeth. "You're supposed to be taking it easy. And we don't even know the course..."

The crowd fell silent as Puzzle cleared a low gate, and then lurched towards the next fence.

He wasn't fast. They had to weave an unusual path as Nicky tried to follow the number order of the course. But once they reached them he cleared them all comfortably. After the first jump, Nicky stopped struggling. He let Puzzle have his head, and enjoy himself.

"And that was the only clear round of this afternoon, which puts Puzzle into first place, followed by Bretta Miles on Eclipse, and Melvyn Leach on Bullet..."

Anything else the announcer might have wanted to say was drowned out by the roar of delight from the crowd.

39

"When does Megan Wise start at Mill Farm?" Tom rattled in, carrying bowls of salad and garlic bread. Through the kitchen door the smell of potatoes baking in the oven wafted after him.

"On Monday." Nicky took the bowls from him and set them down on the table next to Tom's ancient leather chair. "Melvyn Leach wanted Lynette to start working at his place as soon as possible."

"Sssssssh! It's starting." Sabrina glanced round at them both, and nudged up close to Jade on the floor.

"Come and sit down." Bretta wriggled along the carpet, making a space for Nicky.

The five of them were glued to the television as the *Crazy About Creatures* theme tune filled Tom's tiny front room.

Aileen Forbes appeared on the screen suddenly, her teeth still flashing as she stood at the door to the water mill. A man in a dark suit with a notebook was measuring something in the background.

"The response to last week's appeal has been amazing. As you can see, the council has already started putting up silver balls along the power lines, to protect the bird life here…"

The scene changed for a moment, showing a shot of the cable, followed by a close-up of a blackbird singing noisily in a nearby tree.

"… And our water mill museum project has already received a staggering 11,000 aluminium ring pulls. So keep them coming in. With our fund-raising, and the promised council grant, we're hoping to start work by the end of the summer. I spoke to Tom Hughes, the proposed caretaker of the museum, to find out just how far things have come since last week…"

Nicky, Sabrina, Bretta and Jade all turned to smile at Tom as his face filled the screen.

"That can't be me!" he muttered. "I haven't got that many wrinkles, surely?"

"Start washing in mill water," Bretta giggled. "You can even get it bottled and sell it to the public once they start coming round."

"You could say it's the secret to eternal youth," Sabrina added.

Tom gave them both a boyish grin. "We'll see if Patty will pay for the face-lift first. Otherwise no one will be fooled."

The scene swung away from Tom, to close in on Maggie, who was waddling beside him.

Maggie, unimpressed by her moment of stardom, hissed loudly.

"...and as well as attracting all sorts of visitors in the future, the renovation work will provide employment for local builders, carpenters and other workers in the months to come."

Aileen Forbes began to give a slow tour of the inside, pointing out an old turbine shaft, a wooden hopper, and the giant circular millstones that Nicky had sat on when he'd sheltered in the mill. "There are even plans to incorporate craft workshops into the site. So remember – keep those ring-pulls coming in, and we'll give you a week-by-week account of developments here at the old water mill..."

The programme switched to a story about an elderly lady in a yellow straw hat who had just rescued a string of seaside donkeys.

"I won't be long," Nicky whispered to Bretta. "I'm just going outside for ten minutes."

It was early evening. A few streaks of sunset hung in the sky over the water mill. Its dark, gaunt shapes were beautiful in the dying light. Patty had promised the changes would only make it safe, not different. Nicky hoped she was right.

He turned away from the mill, sprang over the five-barred gate into the next field, and made a deep, husky call in his throat. Puzzle, who was grazing peacefully beneath the trees, trotted across, whickering with pleasure.

"Enjoying your holiday?" Nicky whispered, rubbing his forehead. "If I have my way, Patty will rest you for at least a year. Then next season ... who knows? Maybe you'll jump again – or maybe, once the public start coming to the museum, she'll find you're more of an asset here than in the competition ring."

Puzzle blew softly on Nicky's shoulder, and began chewing his sleeve. Nicky hugged him suddenly, then stepped back at a sudden hiss from behind him. Maggie, her beak wide open, was waving her good wing at him jealously.

Nicky grinned down at her. "How's Tom going to feel when he finds out you've fallen in love with someone else?"

Maggie hissed again, and Puzzle stretched down his nose and touched her gently. Maggie let her wing drop back against her side, and settled in the grass between Puzzle's front legs. Puzzle nuzzled her for a moment longer, then dropped his head to graze.

Nicky leant against Puzzle and stood quietly, watching the sky behind Tom's bungalow change from pink, then to orange, and then to gold.

He saw Sabrina appear at the door, and wave.

Nicky waved back. "Looks like supper's ready," he whispered to Puzzle, giving him one last, fierce hug. "It's time for me to go."

Maggie glared at Nicky, but she didn't hiss again.

Nicky turned and sprinted back across the field towards the bungalow.

Don't miss the first title
in the series:

Horse
Healer
Eclipse

1

Every time he went, Nicky knew he was doing something wrong. If he ever got caught, he'd really be for it. Except it didn't *feel* wrong. Not in his heart. It was just that he knew that no one else would ever see it in the same way he did.

He slowed his bike to a halt and wheeled it silently into the bushes, wedging it inside a tangle of brambles so it couldn't be seen from the road.

A black car was coming, travelling fast down the country lane. Nicky ducked down out of sight and waited as it roared past.

As the growl of the engine faded into the distance, Nicky straightened up. Stepping softly out into the open, he vaulted lightly across the five-barred gate. He made no sound as he landed.

Quietly, very quietly, he crept between the cluster of trees that lined the edge of the field.

It was dusk, and already shapes and shadows were beginning to spread towards each other across the silence. The moon was out, but its silver crescent was masked behind heavy grey clouds.

In the dusty half-light Nicky could still make out the horse grazing at the far side of the field. Eclipse, an Arab mare, with a coat so dark that in some lights she looked completely black. She had no other markings except for a partial star on her forehead. And she was beautiful. Nicky loved all horses, but she was something above the others. There was a magic about her, a wildness that drew him to her again and again.

He stood for a long time, letting the darkness settle around him, listening to scratchings and scrabblings that rustled the leaves of the whispering trees.

Nearby a twig snapped. Nicky tensed, his sharp green eyes darting towards the sound. It was only a squirrel scuttering up a nearby tree.

Nicky took a deep breath. He felt odd tonight. Jumpy. But he was stupid to feel jumpy. The night would be spoilt if he was on edge. And he didn't want it spoilt. It was too precious. Too special. He was hungry for the buzz of excitement and the racing energy that Eclipse always gave him.

He stepped forward and, low in his throat, he uttered a call. It was a deep, almost animal sound.

Immediately Eclipse lifted her head, her ears flicking forward as she listened.

Nicky called again and Eclipse began to trot towards him, whickering softly.

She drew up close and for a moment they just stood, watching each other. There was no fear between them. Nicky knew Eclipse and Eclipse knew Nicky. He held out his hand and she nuzzled against him. She wasn't looking for treats or tit-bits. Her action was a simple greeting. A warm welcome.

Nicky touched the half-star on her forehead. It was a light movement, very gentle, but Eclipse understood it. It was a sign – a secret message to reassure her, and to strengthen the trust between them. Then he moved to her side. He ran his hand along her neck and shoulder, then leaned against her, catching the rich, sweet smell of her body.

He sprang up on to her.

He didn't kick, or even push with his knees, and although his hands touched the rich silk of her mane, he didn't hold on.

"Walk." He spoke gently, almost whispering, yet Eclipse responded immediately, arching her neck and stepping out proudly as she moved forwards. This was the moment Nicky always loved best, the moving together as if they were almost one animal.

"Now trot." Squeezing with his legs, Nicky guided Eclipse round in a perfect figure of eight, first one way, and then the other. A quiet word made her stop instantly, her nostrils flared and her neck arched. Another squeeze and she was cantering, moving like a dream horse, with a floating grace that had a magic all of its own.

Suddenly Eclipse jumped sideways, rearing up slightly with her ears laid back.

"What the hell do you think you're doing?" A torch beam flashed across Nicky's face. Eclipse snorted and tossed her head.

"Easy. Easy," Nicky murmured. Eclipse stood silent, but her head stayed raised and watchful. She was ready to run if she had to.

Nicky twisted towards the glare, squinting. Even in the darkness he could see the girl. Thin. Scruffy. Shoulder-length brown hair tucked back behind her ears. It couldn't have been worse. It was Bretta Miles, a girl from his class at school.

"Can't you stop waving that torch about? You're frightening the horse."

"*I'm* frightening the horse!" Bretta spoke with an indignant squeal. "Well, I'd love to know what you must be doing, leaping about on her in the dead of night."

"I'm not leaping about. I'm working her quietly."

"But not for long, I bet. You've been here before

haven't you, riding her at night? I've noticed she's been different some mornings. Sweated up and excited. I bet you've been galloping her and everything."

Nicky didn't answer, but Bretta was right. Eclipse had given him some beautiful night rides, racing the moon down the length of the field, or sometimes riding through into the outdoor school where the jumps were always set up.

"You'd better get off, anyway. You're trespassing, and stealing, and all sorts of other things."

For a wild moment, Nicky thought about urging Eclipse on and galloping away. But it wouldn't have done him any good. Bretta would only go running to Edward Carter. Edward was in Nicky's class too. He was friends with Bretta, *and* he owned Eclipse. Between them they wouldn't waste a second before calling the police – or the "gavvers", as Gypsies called them.

A visit from the law was something that Nicky, and the rest of his family, could do without.

He jumped to the ground and Bretta put her hand on the horse's side, walking all round her, checking her legs and hooves with the torch.

"I haven't hurt her. I don't hurt horses. I don't hurt any animals."

"That's not what I've heard."

Nicky stiffened. He knew what Bretta was

hinting at. She was talking about the petition the locals had all signed after some newspaper bloke had come sniffing round their site taking photographs. After that people had started complaining because Nicky's family kept their Alsatian dog Sky tied up outside the trailer.

"She's not tied up all the time," Nicky flashed back. "But she's a guard dog. She's got a job to do, and it's what she was trained for. She's probably happier than some sad little lap dog with ribbons in its coat."

"She shouldn't be tied up at all," Bretta retorted. "Animals need to be free."

Once again, Nicky didn't answer. In a way she was right. But they couldn't let Sky loose when they weren't around. She might wander off and get blamed for worrying sheep or something. And they couldn't keep her inside either. Most Gypsies never allowed animals inside their trailers. It would be dirty. Unhygienic. Nicky knew that the gorgios (anyone who didn't have Gypsy blood) didn't seem to worry about things like that, but this probably wasn't a good time to let Bretta Miles know what he thought about house-dwellers' living standards.

His fingers dug suddenly into Eclipse's side, making her flinch and back away in surprise. "Sky's on a long rope," he muttered, "and she can go under the trailer if she's too hot, or if it's wet. We have to keep her there to protect the trailer anyway – to stop people sneaking up and causing trouble for us…"

"A bit like you then. Sneaking out here and riding someone else's horse. That's causing trouble too. If Edward knew you'd been here, riding Eclipse…"

Nicky stared across at Bretta through the darkness. "Does that mean you're not going to tell him?" He hated having to ask. He hated being under Bretta's control like this. But more than that he hated the thought of Edward knowing. Ever since Christmas, when Nicky first started at Maybridge School, Edward never missed an opportunity to jeer or pick on him.

"I ought to tell him." Bretta ran her fingertips over Eclipse, searching for cuts or lumps. "But I'm supposed to be here helping him – looking after Eclipse because Edward can't at the moment. And I really think he's got enough on his plate without worrying that you might be out here, creeping around, don't you?"

Nicky pushed his hands deep into his pockets and stayed quiet.

"Now you'd better get out of here," Bretta spat suddenly, "before you upset Eclipse even more." She circled her arms round the horse's neck, leaning against her and stroking her nose. "Come on, girl. It's OK. You'll be all right now."

But it was Nicky Eclipse was watching as he walked away.

And as Nicky reached the gate and sprang across, Eclipse neighed suddenly, a loud, shrill sound that split the night.

It was as if she was calling to him.